He could have saved them.

When a hurricane ripped through Florida last year, it leveled high school student Jim Beauregard's house—while his mom and sister were trapped inside.

Now "home" is a FEMA trailer, shared with his overweight and disabled aunt. Facing eviction, Jim's got to earn enough money for a new place, fast. But when he loses his construction job after being duped by his nemesis, Hollis Mulwray, Jim's got nothing left. Only by joining an underground gambling ring does he see a glimmer of hope—in a roomful of dangerous (and possibly crazy) older men.

And more could be at stake than he realizes.

The Straits

Jeremy Craig

The Straits

flux™
Woodbury, Minnesota

First Edition
First Printing, 2009

Book design by Steffani Sawyer
Cover design by Gavin Dayton Duffy
Cover images © 2009 iStockphoto.com

Flux, an imprint of Llewellyn Publications

Library of Congress Cataloging-in-Publication Data
Craig, Jeremy, 1979–
　The Straits / Jeremy Craig.—1st ed.
　　p. cm.
　Summary: After his mother and sister are killed in Hurricane Leland, fifteen-year-old Jim tries to find solace and financial stability through gambling.
　ISBN 978-0-7387-1444-8
　[1. Gambling—Fiction. 2. Grief—Fiction. 3. Hurricanes—Fiction.] I. Title.
　PZ7.C844188St 2009
　[Fic]—dc22
　　　　　　　　　　　　　　　2009001688

Flux
Llewellyn Publications
A Division of Llewellyn Worldwide, Ltd.
2143 Wooddale Drive, Dept. 978-0-7387-1444-8
Woodbury, MN 55125-2989, U.S.A.
www.fluxnow.com

Printed in the United States of America

To Emily

Like the sparrows of the field,
so are the poor, the powerless and the savage
who would rise up and fly
were there wings to lift them.

Goddamnit, we should've never been there. The only reason we'd stayed behind after the mayor issued the evacuation was because of Aunt Mel. She was adamant about not leaving town, stubbornly believing that she could just ride out the hurricane like she had "ridden them out in the past." My mom had gone to get Aunt Mel, because of course her house was flooded and she was trapped upstairs or something.

I know it was basically impossible for my mom to leave me and my sister, Martha, but she did what she had to. She stuffed us in the closet because it was structurally the safest place in the house and told us to stay down and not to come out for anything, "not anything, do you hear me!" Then she slammed the door on us and drove away to rescue Aunt Mel.

Not long after she left, the roof roared up and split and flipped skyward and longways, splintering into shards as it wrapped against a palm tree in the front yard. High above the house was a telephone pole and the wires from the large cylindrical base were sparkling. It was directly above our heads, shaking dangerously. I knew that if it fell, it would've probably collapsed the entire house and definitely crush us to death.

I wrapped my arms around Martha and told her to follow me and "don't let go of my hand, not for anything, do you hear me!"

"Okay, but don't leave me!" she cried.

"I won't, I promise!"

I thought we should get to the kitchen pantry because that part of the roof was still intact and it was the nearest thing to a closet that seemed safe.

I helped Martha to her feet and we were off.

We ran as fast as we could, through the house, or what was left of it, toward the kitchen. As we passed through the living room, I saw my mom pull up in the car, alone, and slam on the breaks, skidding several feet across the flooded grass before stopping.

We bolted outside.

Running around the front of the car, my mom looked relieved and worried at the same time. And then I realized that I wasn't holding Martha's hand, that she wasn't with me. I had left her behind.

"Where's your sister?" she shouted.

My heart was beating so hard and fast. Hard and fast.

She shook her head, worried. "Go to the car!" she continued.

Hard and fast.

"No, I wanna go with you!" I yelled.

"GO TO THE CAR!"

I leapt off the porch and sprinted across the corner of the yard. It was only fifteen or twenty feet, but with the hurricane in full force and all, it was the hardest and longest fifteen or twenty feet of my life. A good bet I was going to get blown away or swept up by the goddamn deluge that was destroying the neighborhood if I didn't hurry.

I crashed down into the front seat of the car and slammed the door shut. Everything went silent, like the bottom of the deep, dark ocean. Truthfully, who knew if the bottom of the ocean was really silent or not, that's just what my mom used to say when it was late at night and she wanted me and Martha to be quiet and stop kidding around and "for the last time, go to sleep already." She'd put her hands on her hips and say, "in three seconds, I want this room like the bottom of the deep, dark ocean." She liked poetry and crap so she used metaphors, similes and such whenever she had the opportunity. And when those didn't work, she'd use the wooden paddle that she kept near her bedside table.

In one quick glimpse, I surveyed what was left of the neighborhood and it wasn't much, let me tell you: abandoned houses with walls and roofs buckled in or crudely ripped apart; palm trees shaking and contorting in the wind; deserted cars protruding halfway out of the muddy water like gravestones in a cemetery. I hardly recognized the place where I had spent the last ten years of my life. I hardly recognized it.

I looked back at our house. I knew my mom was inside frantically searching for Martha, running from room to room, shouting her name. "Martha!" And I envisioned her opening and slamming doors. "Martha!" Turning over furniture looking for her. "Martha!" And I imagined Martha, left behind in the earsplitting darkness, alone and crying with no one to hear.

There was no way to know any of this for sure, but it was pretty easy to figure out based on the situation. Kinda like in card playing. If you know what cards you have, what cards are showing, based on how your opponent has been betting you can take a pretty decent guess at what's in their hand and know if you're gonna come out on top or not. For one thing, I knew how much my mom loved Martha and me, and I knew that she would gladly go through hell or high water for us—twice—so I could guess that she was in there going nuts trying to find Martha. And I knew Martha well enough to know that she was probably wandering around, making it more difficult to be found by my mom.

Of course, betting isn't an exact science, and any number of things can go wrong and for some of us, they usually do.

Suddenly, I saw Martha appear in the kitchen window. She was looking out at me. There was fear and confusion in her eyes because she was alone in the house and I was outside in the car. And it was all my fault because I let go of her hand.

I had abandoned her because I never could do anything right.

We stared at each other for what seemed like minutes. It was probably only a few seconds. I tried to move, but my body was heavy and sluggish, like it didn't want to do what I wanted it to.

Struggling against myself, I finally got out of the car and stood behind the door, unable to go any farther. I wanted more than anything to run inside and grab Martha and find mom, but I was paralyzed by the fear.

As I stood behind the car door, getting pummeled by the howling wind and rain, something weird caught my eye. I looked away from Martha to see a little brown sparrow sitting on part of the porch frame. The bird just looked at me and cocked its head. Then, it took flight and vanished into the storm. Like it was never there. I had no idea where that bird came from or where it went or what the living hell it might have been doing on a railing in the middle of a hurricane. It could've been just my imagination, but since I believed in God and fate and supernatural stuff and since I believed in goddamn miracles—even if I didn't act like it all the time—I thought that little sparrow had something special to do with it.

At that very moment, in a loud spark and roar of twisted metal and broken wood, the telephone pole crashed down on top of the house. I ducked behind the car door as the remaining walls and roof sagged and collapsed in front me, burying Martha and mom beneath the smoking and soggy rubble of the house. I felt my muscles contract and that strange queasiness overcome me, like I had been sucked into the endless shadowy corridors of one of my mom's bedtime similes—because everything was still and silent, like the bottom of the deep, dark ocean.

And then, through the silence, someone called my name. "Jim! Hey, Jim, what the hell're you looking at?"

Almost One Year Later

WEDNESDAY AFTERNOON, AUGUST 27

The 53rd Weather Reconnaissance Squadron/403rd Wing, based at Keesler Air Force Base in Biloxi, Mississippi, records the development of a severe thunderstorm off the west coast of Africa.

The radar begins tracking the storm's progress as it moves westward at 30 mph.

One

Jim Beauregard! What're you doing up there?" someone yelled. I was standing on the Andersons' roof peering down through a shaftway five floors into the dark basement. It was a long way to fall and a lot longer for someone like me who was afraid of heights.

I loathed being on the roof of the Andersons' house, but Harbinger, my boss, had told me to "stop worrying about how high it is, you woodpecker, and get the hell up there and start laying down those shingles because there is work to be done, *Bogart.*" Harbinger always called me by my last name, which he didn't even know how to correctly pronounce. Harbinger was an idiot.

I adjusted the safety rope and carefully turned around and saw Jackson getting out of his car.

He drove a hand-me-down blue station wagon that had wood paneling, part of which was missing. And it was the ugliest thing you ever saw. A big car that was nice looking was one thing. A big car that was ugly, well, that was just one enormous reminder of how unfair life really was. I never made fun of Jackson's car, though, not to his face anyway. For two reasons: first, I didn't even have a car and that set the bar pretty low for what I could and couldn't make fun of, and secondly, Jackson had anger management issues that I wasn't all that keen on getting to the bottom of.

Once, I think he assumed I was making fun of the station wagon when I asked him if, as a kid, he had ever ridden in that farthest rear seat that faces backwards. I told him how that would embarrass the hell out of me. He didn't say anything for a while, and when he did finally say something, it wasn't to tell me if he had ridden in the farthest back seat.

"What the hell do you think I'm doing up here?" I shouted back.

Jackson was standing in the middle of the yard, looking up, shielding his eyes from the sun. "When do you get off work?"

"I'm supposed to go to class later, but nothing else." We were shouting at each other. "Why, what's going on?" I asked.

"I wanted to finish our conversation, you know, from last night. Can you take a break?"

"Sure," I said. I was the only one on the job site. Of course I could take a break.

"Cool, I'm coming up," Jackson yelled excitedly and ran into the garage. I slowly inched away from the edge of the roof and sat down next to a block of the storm-proof shingles that Harbinger was always bragging about to prospective clients.

The Andersons' house was in the midst of a pretty large renovation project. My employer, Mulwray Construction, LLC (family owned and operated since 1974), had been hired to beautify it and, throughout the summer, I'd been sporadically assigned to work on the place—redoing the floors, rounding out the corners, menial tasks like that. I was just skilled enough to do all of the jobs that nobody else wanted to do. And that's why I was standing on the roof in the middle of a subtropical August heat wave.

My ass could feel the heat radiating from the roof through my jeans. I took my T-shirt off and sat on it and leaned back against my elbows.

Jackson emerged from the open attic window. He was out of breath. "I gotta quit smoking soon," he said. Jackson said that every time he needed an excuse for not being a very good athlete. Like, whenever we played basketball or whatever and he inevitably sucked because he was out of shape, he'd say, "I gotta quit smoking."

Jackson Crawford was eighteen years old and he had

one of those round, well-meaning faces. He also had a gap in his two front teeth. It was pretty big, but it didn't look all that bad. He was real sensitive about his smile, though. About four months ago, I saw him take one of those miniature baseball bats that you get at baseball games to someone's van after the owner made some remark about how his smile looked like a tuning fork.

As he took off his shirt and sat down next to me, he noticed the safety rope that was tied around my waist. "Nice seat belt."

"Shut up."

"Doesn't your boss know that you're afraid of heights?" he asked.

"Yeah," I said.

"He put you up here on purpose? That's hilarious."

"Freaking hilarious."

Jackson clicked his tongue and then said, "So what're *you* doing tonight?"

He was being cagey—he obviously had something in mind. "Probably not whatever you're thinking."

"Well, remember when I came by your trailer last night?" he began.

I did remember. It had been the middle of the night. "What do you want?" I had asked him as I slid my bedroom window up.

"I need your help."

I'd looked at my alarm clock. It was two in the morning.

"I'm in trouble," he'd said as he lit a cigarette and leaned against the window. Our trailer was elevated on cinder blocks, so he was a foot or so below me. I thought he was behaving pretty casually for being in big trouble and it being in the middle of the night and all.

"Trouble? Did you lose your watch, and why aren't you wearing a shirt?" Jackson didn't have a shirt on.

"I was hot," he explained. "Now listen, I need your help at cards."

"You're standing here in the middle of the night half naked. Any help you need at playing cards might not be your biggest problem."

"Hardy, har, har," he joked. "Well, what do you say? You going to help me?"

"I say go away," I replied. "I'll see you tomorrow or something."

"No," he said as he began climbing up and in through the window. "It can't wait."

"What the hell?" I pushed him back out. "Hold on."

"This is serious. I need your help."

He was standing half in the moonlight and half in shadow and I thought that was awfully appropriate, because that's how Jackson was. He seemed like a good guy most of the time.

"You don't get good at cards in five minutes, man. It takes time. Practice."

"Got all night," he said.

"I'm kinda busy sleeping here. We'll talk tomorrow." I shut the window and went back to bed.

Now I leaned forward and rested my arms against my knees. The sun had disappeared behind a large cloud. "Does this have anything to do with why last night was the first time I've seen you around the Straits in days?" I asked. "Because folks have been wondering where the hell their ride to town has been."

The trailer park where I lived was called the Straits. It was kind of out in the middle of nowhere, a good drive from town. And even though Jackson didn't live there, he usually was around almost every day because he used his station wagon as a taxi to give folks without cars of their own lifts between the trailer park and downtown Ambricourt.

He snickered. "I can see them all waiting there by the front gate, sweating and cursing me," he said.

"You don't feel bad about that?"

"Why should *I* have to take them to town?"

"Because you gave them the expectation that you would. Oh, I get it, you don't think we're worth your time, just cause we live in the Straits, right? You can just do whatever you want." What bothered me more than anything—anything in the world—was folks who thought that they were more important or better than others just because they had a car or a big house or whatever.

"That's not what I'm saying," he defended himself.

"Yeah, it is. Otherwise, you wouldn't be here right now. You'd be giving them rides."

"Fine, I'm sorry. Shit, relax. I didn't drive all the way over here to discuss the ethical responsibilities I have to my customers. Why're you in such a bad mood?"

"I dunno," I said. "Maybe because I didn't get much sleep last night. Or maybe cause I don't like being on this roof. And it's hot as hell. Or maybe because Aunt Mel and I only got til Monday to find a new place to live."

"All valid points," he stated. "I would say that you could come live with my family, but we don't have space."

"Thanks. Whatever, it doesn't matter."

We sat there for a few seconds in silence watching a car slowly turn around the cul-de-sac.

"Sorry about getting mad," I offered.

"Don't worry about it. So, what do you say about helping me out?"

I pulled out my deck of cards and shuffled them a couple of times with one hand, as fast as I could. I was kind of showing off, but I dropped some of the cards on the roof. One or two almost slid off. I grabbed them up quickly.

"Maybe you're *not* the one I should be dealing with," he said, pulling out a cigarette and putting it in his mouth. He left it there, unlit.

"Like I said last night, you're not going to get good at playing cards just like that, y'know."

"How'd you get so good at cards?"

"Uh, I've played a lot." That was the truth. Ever since I could remember I'd been playing cards, either with my sister or by myself or with someone else. Most of my earliest memories, for better or worse, have something to do with a deck of cards. "You'd get better if you played more," I said.

"Which is why I'd like you to play and win *for* me."

"First of all, with what money? Second of all, who is going to let some fifteen-year-old in a game?"

Jackson looked out across the neighborhood and then said real solemn-like, "Over the past several weeks, I've come to grips with the harsh reality that I'm just not that good at gambling."

"I could have told you that a long time ago."

"I'm serious, Jim."

I seriously wasn't going to be able to get out of at least talking about it with him. "Where's the game?"

"It floats," he explained. "But lately, the racket's been down on Sycamore Street. One of the abandoned houses there."

The Sycamore Street district was a thirty-minute drive from the Straits, on the opposite side of town.

"Racket? What're you, some kind of Johnny Mafia type all of a sudden? I didn't even know people were still living in that neighborhood."

"They're not. It's basically deserted and that's why we're playing there. Before, the game was at the Drysdale, and then after the cops busted it up, it was moved to Sycamore. The guy just started the parlor a few months ago."

"What game have you been playing?"

"What do you think?" Jackson asked.

"Texas Hold'em?"

"The Cadillac. If it's good enough for the World Series, I guess it's good enough for me," he said as he lit his cigarette and flashed his gap-filled grin.

Two

I liked Texas Hold'em because not only did I get to say a lot of cool words, like *flop, turn, river, pocket, hole, big blind,* and *small blind,* but also it was the first poker game I learned how to play. And because it's pretty simple, too: each player is dealt two cards face down. Those two cards are called *preflop* cards because you get them before *the flop.* After looking at their preflop cards, each player can either fold or play by betting the ante. After everyone has decided to play (or not), three cards from the deck are played face up for everyone to see. That's called the flop. Those cards are community cards and can be combined with each person's two private (preflop) cards to make the best five-card hand. After another round of betting, where folks can check, call, fold, or raise—just like most other poker games—another community card is turned over, called *the turn*. Just like before, there's another round of betting (or folding, calling, and checking). After the last community card (called *the river*) is turned over (bringing the total number of face-up cards to five), all the players who haven't folded show their cards and the best five-card hand wins.

"So who runs the game?" I asked, taking one of Jackson's cigarettes and lighting it. If Aunt Mel found out that I was smoking, she'd kill me.

"This guy," Jackson said. "They call him Robert. I guess he travels around from town to town, setting up shop wherever he can get away with it."

"So why Ambricourt?"

"I asked him the same question. He said, 'who in Ambricourt doesn't want to get rich quick? And those who *are* rich definitely have the money to lose it.'"

We both agreed that Robert had a pretty good point.

Jackson stood up and moved closer to the edge of the roof. He spit off and watched his spit fall to the concrete below. Splat.

"Could you not do that?" I said. "My lunch is down there."

"Sorry."

"Anyway," I continued. "What made you think you could walk into some floating parlor game and win?"

He wiped his mouth with the back of his arm. "I didn't tolerate two years of high school to be a cab driver. And my car hasn't been running good lately. Something's wrong with it and if it breaks down, I'm screwed like you, working out here on this roof in scorching August."

"That's not my problem. You could go get a normal job."

"I've never worked a normal job in my life. I'm not going to start now."

"How much are you down?" I pressed, having saved perhaps the most obvious question for last.

He plopped back down next to me. It was clear he didn't want to answer. He sighed and said, "I had to take a loan from a friend of a friend. He wants his money back with interest."

"What the hell were you thinking?" I asked. "The first rule of gambling is not to bet what you can't lose."

"Rules are made to be broken," he joked.

"And look what happens, dumbass," I snapped back. "I mean, I'm not one to judge, but—"

"Then don't," he said sharply. "It's not like you've never been busted for gambling."

I knew exactly what he was referring to. *Exactly.* "Don't bring that up," I responded. "That's totally different."

"How?"

"Hollis set me up."

"That's what they all say."

"Whatever. You know he framed me to take the fall for that bullshit."

Jackson didn't immediately respond. Then he shrugged and said, "I know."

I felt real sorry for him, sitting there on the roof of the Andersons' house. On the surface he looked confident and self-assured. But the devil was in the details. I'd noticed his hand shaking, ever so slightly, when he was holding that cigarette. And there was a certain weakness to his voice, a feeble tremor in the back of his throat that I'd never heard before. Those were his *tells*—little signs indicating what was going on in his head. He was sending signals all over the place even though he didn't intend to. In a card game, the smallest things—an indiscriminate glance, a move of the hand, a twitch—send the biggest signals. No wonder he lost all his money at cards, I thought.

"You're sure you can get me into the game?"

"Yeah."

"Then what am I going to buy in with? I don't have any money."

He hesitated before answering. "What about that money you and Aunt Mel keep in your trailer."

"I told you about that?" I was surprised to be confronted with my own indiscretion.

"What, it's not like I'm going to steal it or anything," he said.

"I know. But I can't use that. It's all we have."

"Come on, Jim. Please. If I don't pay this guy back, I don't know what he'll do and it's not like you have to use all of it, just some. And I've been driving your ass around all summer. Please, Jim."

I knew it was a bad idea, but he did need my help. "You'll owe me," I said. "And I'm out of the game once we get your money back."

"Fine."

"I can't afford to get wrapped up in some gambling scheme again," I pressed, driving home the point.

"Fine."

"'Cause with everything going on, that's about the last thing I need," I continued.

"Jim! I get it already."

Jackson left as rain began to fall. I went inside and got something to drink before grabbing a couple of books from Mr. Anderson's study and going to the garage to wait out the weather. I sat on an old stereo box with the garage door open, looking at the different pictures and waiting for the rain to stop. It was humid in there, but not hot. Musty. The rain fell and the thunder boomed.

The storm abated after a while, and I went back up to the roof. I was working for about an hour before Hollis Mulwray ruined my perfectly forgettable day by showing up.

Three

Hollis' arrival at any job site pretty much signaled the impending destruction or ruination of something. Like this one time, at the beginning of summer, during my first couple of days on the job, I was working at this big house in this really paunchy neighborhood. Like he usually does, Hollis showed up unannounced without anything specific to do, so he went exploring, tracking mud throughout the house. I followed his footprints into the living room, up the stairs, and down the hallway—I felt like I was tracking some wild game or something—and into a bedroom at the end of the hall. The muddy footprints led straight to Hollis, who was going through some girl's underwear drawer.

Seventeen and pretty well built, Hollis was taller than me. He had dark, spiked hair, which he prided himself on keeping perfectly shaped and faded—he was constantly touching it and patting it back into place. He probably used an entire bottle of gel on it every morning.

"Hollis!" I'd said, scaring him half out of his dimwits. I could see his porcupine hair shake in place as he jumped and turned around.

"Look, you sexual predator," I pointed to the tracks.

"Whoops," he observed as he hurriedly stuffed the panties back in the drawer.

"We need to clean it up before they get home!"

He smiled. "I don't," he said smugly. "You do."

Since Hollis' family owned the construction company, I really wasn't in too much of a position to go causing a stir about anything. Decent paying summer jobs were somewhat of a rarity in Ambricourt and I didn't want to give them a reason to fire me, something I'm sure Hollis desperately wanted to happen.

So as Hollis entertained himself with an Otter Pop, I got the mud cleaned up except for this one spot on a rug, but I just flipped it over so nobody would notice.

Even though I was lucky to have a job and a roof over my head, I tried not to think about how great some kids had it. But it was hard sometimes not to compare myself to guys like Hollis, who seemed to have everything he could ever want—the perfect family, a nice car, popularity, a big house…I had none of those things, so let me tell you, it was hard not to be jealous sometimes.

That day, early in the summer, he had bragged on and on, telling me every little thing about what had been going on at the Academy since I left, even about the new English teacher that had replaced my mom. He said that he'd been occasionally going out with a girl from my grade, Vera Danner, and he told me about some of their sexual exploits. He even used that word, "exploits." Vera was one of those girls who had a large and well-documented sexual history, so I didn't know who was exploiting whom in that relationship, but there was definitely some of it going on.

"What do you want?" I asked Hollis now, as he climbed out onto the roof.

"Just checking up on you before my hot date with Kathy."

"Uh-huh." I said, sarcastically. I knew he was lying, just to piss me off. He only wished Kathy were going out with him.

"How's *dummer* school?" he asked snidely.

"How's sitting around on your ass?"

"Like that's all I do," he replied.

I'm not sure Hollis actually did any work for his grandfather's company, but he did find the time in his exceedingly busy schedule to check in on me—at least a couple of times a week. See, after the last hurricane, there was plenty of construction work to be done. So much so that Mulwray Construction wasn't too picky in who they hired. And that's why I got the job, not because I was overly qualified or anything, but because I knew which side of the hammer was supposed to hit the nail. Boy, I wish I could've been there to see the look on Hollis' scrawny face when he found out that his nemesis was on his grandfather's payroll.

Hollis glanced down the shaftway and whistled. "A long way down," he said. "I'd hate for you to fall." He spit a wad of chewing tobacco down. Then he turned around and looked at me.

"That's why I've got this on," I said as I held up the safety rope.

"What good is that going to do?"

"What good do you think?"

"I dunno," he said as he pulled the safety rope out through the window. He'd obviously loosened it from the crossbeam I'd secured it to. The blood washed out of my face and I got safely down on my hands and knees. He just stood there laughing at me. "Listen, Jim," he said, as if he was about to impart a piece of earthly wisdom he probably stole from someone else. "As you may or may not know, the Wilmots' party is Friday and I just want to remind you that no trailer trash is allowed. Don't get mad at me, I didn't make the rule."

"Remind me why I would want to go that stupid-ass party when I don't even go to school with you all anymore."

Hollis stared at me, and then smiled and patted his sculpted hair. He said, "Just making sure."

"That's why you stopped by, to make sure I wasn't going to that party?"

"And to tell you to stay away from Kathy."

"What?"

"You heard me."

"Kathy can be friends with whoever she wants."

"But you can't."

"Whatever," I said.

"It's in your best interest to stay away from her, or else."

"Or else what?" I challenged.

"Find out." He stared at me until I looked away.

I hated Hollis. He thought he was better than everyone just 'cause he was rich.

"I bet this house has a deck of cards somewhere..." he continued.

"Don't even think about it," I snapped.

"What're you? Afraid?"

"No, I just remember what happened the last time we played. I got expelled. And don't think that I don't know you paid everyone to say it was me who started it."

The side of Hollis' mouth curled slowly. "Come on, then, if you think you're such a badass."

"What's in it for me?" I asked.

"What do you want?"

"Aside from you to leave me alone?"

"I can do that if you win," he said.

I really wanted to play him.

"Fine, how about this," he said as he pulled out two twenty-dollar bills. "I'll give you this twenty, so it's a free game for you. If I win, I get my money back, if you win, you get forty bucks."

I thought about it. I *was* bored as hell. And I knew I could win. He was a lot worse than he gave himself credit for. And Aunt Mel and I could use forty bucks. "No," I said.

"Oh, come on, Bogart, grow a pair. It's not like your mom's here to do anything about it."

At hearing Hollis mention her, I wanted to push him off the roof. "We'll use shingles for chips," I said angrily, pulling out my deck of cards.

We played right there on the roof. Not surprisingly, it only took a few hands to take Hollis *all in*. Reading him was like reading one of Martha's kid books. Whenever he had a good hand, he underbet, trying to lure me into calling. Whenever he bet big, he was bluffing—it didn't get any easier than that.

On the last hand, my pocket cards were a king and a jack of clubs.

The flop was a three, four, and seven of diamonds.

Hollis checked, allowing me the chance to make the first move. I figured he had either flopped a flush or had a flush draw. I raised him big—four shingles—thinking that if he called me, he didn't have a flush after all.

So it went back to Hollis. And what do you know, he called, so I turned over the fourth card—another king. I had two kings against his possible flush. He tossed in five dollars worth of shingles.

I was having trouble getting a read on him this time, although I was pretty sure he didn't have a flush. He just wanted me to think he did.

"All in," I said.

He thought about it and then said, "call."

He flipped over his pocket cards. He only had one diamond, which meant he only had a flush draw.

I flipped over my king and jack. I was in a pretty good spot. The only way for him to beat me was to snag a diamond on the river.

"A flush beats two kings," he said just for the hell of it.

"*If* you get a flush," I corrected.

I burned one card and turned over the last card, the river card—a beautiful ace of clubs! The loss registered on his face immediately.

"Two kings beats your flush draw," I said with a smug laugh. "Thanks for the forty bucks, bitch." I took the two twenties and stuffed them in one pocket and my deck of cards in the other. "Still the best."

"Shut up, you just got lucky."

"No, I *just* got your money," I replied. "And I'm not trailer trash, you dickhead."

Hollis stood up and climbed back in through the window. "Follow me, Bogart."

Four

I didn't always hate Hollis so much. Several years ago, we were actually friends. But we had one of those friendships that only existed because we had something in common—cards. You take that one thing away, and we didn't have much of a relationship.

He was a year older and a grade above me, and back in seventh and eighth grade we'd play at lunch and on breaks—whenever we were together and had a spare moment. We had to be pretty discreet about the whole thing cause the Academy thoroughly disapproved of playing cards or gambling on school property. We could never get a big game going because a crowd of boys huddling around the fence at recess drew a healthy amount of suspicion. Mostly it was just Hollis and me or maybe one other person who we trusted. Although the poker games started as mere entertainment, they quickly escalated into something else entirely: playing for lunch money, favors, and homework assignments.

This would have been fine had Hollis not been one of those kids who was always getting into trouble, yet miraculously finding a way out of it unscathed. Like the time when I was in eighth grade, when he deliberately made little Jeffrey Steele faint. Jeffrey was a seventh grader who, as it turned out, was pretty sickly.

We were in the boy's bathroom at lunch. Jeffrey entered and without saying exactly why, Hollis coaxed him into hunching over and taking a number of really deep breaths. Then, after Jeffrey stood up, Hollis pressed really hard on his chest. It all happened so fast, I didn't even know what the hell what was going on. The quick loss of air and lack of oxygen to Jeffrey's brain caused him to pass out and hit his head on the hand dryer on the way down.

Hollis actually got in trouble for that one, but so did I, because I was there. My mom said that I "should've stopped him or left because after all, if you don't have your reputation, you don't have anything." Unless you have the reputation of having nothing. In which case, you're totally screwed.

Nobody knew that Jeffrey had a bone disease. But word got out about his bone problem, all right, when Hollis and the English teacher's kid cracked Jeffrey Steele's sternum in the boy's bathroom. But anyway, who expected a kid with the last name Steele to have brittle bones? Poor Jeffrey had to wear this immobile, futuristic chest brace for nine weeks. He looked like a robot walking around the halls with that thing on.

Hollis and I stopped hanging out near the end of my ninth grade year. It wasn't so much that we stopped being friends as we became enemies. Basically what happened was that Hollis had this big idea of starting this secret, middle-stakes gambling ring involving more students than he could safely assume could keep a secret. I had a bad feeling about it, but somehow Hollis managed to convince me to get involved. Well, eventually word got out to the teachers and then you can imagine what all happened after that. It was a huge fiasco that even made the local newspaper. The headline read something like, "GAMBLING RING DISCOVERED AT PRESTIGIOUS ACADEMY. EXPULSIONS EXPECTED." You'd think we had fused an atom or something. It was all pretty innocent, really, but it didn't look so good for the reputation of the hoity-toity Ambricourt Academy.

Although I couldn't prove it, I know the whole operation was a master plan by Hollis—to set me up to take the fall so that I'd get expelled. Hollis had the biggest ego in the world, and he wanted to be best at everything, including cards. As long as I was there, he wasn't.

I tried to tell the administration that Hollis was behind

the gambling ring, but nobody listened and so finally I got tired of talking about it. His family was rich and well respected in the community and I came from a broken charity case of a home that was barely able to make ends meet. You do the goddamn math.

In the end, just like Hollis wanted, I was expelled from the Academy and had to finish up my classes from home—everyone knows that being home-schooled is the modern equivalent to having leprosy. I'm talking Old Testament leprosy. Later that summer, however, my mom petitioned the board and, to my surprise, they let me back in on probation.

That fall, back at the Academy, Hollis tried pretty successfully to make my life hell. He still attempted to get me expelled which, for the second time, would have definitely been for good (two strikes, you're out!). Once he even put on a ski mask and beat some kid up and had one of his upperclass cronies call him by my name. So the kid thought it was me! Fortunately, at the time, I had an airtight alibi—I was in class. By nobody's standard was Hollis brilliant.

I'd been relieved and really happy to be readmitted back at the Academy 'cause of how happy it made my mom feel. More than anything, I wanted to make it all up to her. I knew she was pretty ashamed of the whole ordeal, because she had always tried so hard to raise Martha and me with good morals and integrity and character and crap like that. She said that she was trying to give us everything that she didn't have when she was our age—love, structure, a good home, and a good education.

Sometimes I thought she tried too hard to give us all of those things, because it felt like her being a parent was getting in the way of her being a mother, if that makes any sense. Especially when I got expelled—because for all that I'd done wrong, I just wanted to hear her say it was going to be all right. But she didn't. She was too concerned with trying to make sure I never did anything so patently stupid again.

Five

The Andersons' backyard was beautifully landscaped. It looked like one of those Mediterranean gardens that you see in *National Geographic* or in one of those landscaping magazines or something. There were neat mounds of wood chips where perfectly trimmed hedges sprouted up around manicured palm trees, Magnolias and lemon trees and orange trees. Spotting the lush, sodded grass were various citrus fruits that had fallen from the trees.

As we arrived around back, Hollis picked up an orange and pegged the fence for no apparent reason.

We stopped in the middle of the yard.

"Start digging."

"Huh?"

"Harbinger said, 'tell Bogart to dig up the septic tank.' It's got a corroded interior wall or something."

"What's that?"

"Does it really matter, Bogart?"

"It's just that Harbinger is usually the one who gives me my assignments."

"Fine," Hollis snapped. "Do what you want. Harbinger will be by later and you can explain why you didn't do your job. And then you can get fired. Just don't blame it on me…like everything else."

"Well, I don't see any leakage from the tank," I replied. "Shouldn't that crap be seeping up through the grass or something?"

"Obviously not," he said as he turned and walked around the side of the house, disappearing and leaving me in the backyard with only the oranges and lemons to keep me company. It was just as well that he was gone 'cause even though I had more questions for him, he was probably out of answers anyway.

So I started shoveling and piling, shoveling and piling, shoveling and piling.

Six

Shoveling and piling. Shoveling and piling. Before I knew it, I hit concrete. I think I just sorta zoned out or something; the monotony of digging had been hypnotizing in a way. Just for fun, I had started counting how many digs it took to get to the septic tank. I stopped counting about halfway down, so I don't know how many spadefuls it took. A lot.

Two things happened really fast. I hit the concrete tank with the shovel. And then sewage started leaking and bubbling out. It stunk to high heaven. It wasn't like a geyser or anything, but it was definitely puddling right there in the hole, which I had jumped out of as quickly as possible.

I quickly started shoveling dirt down into the hole. I thought if I could fill it in and cover it and make it look like nobody had been digging there, I might get away with it. I could just play dumb. The puddle of shit and piss was really starting to fill up. I threw shovelfuls of dirt down in there as fast as I could.

And then I heard Harbinger's truck roar to a stop in front of the house.

I knew I was done for.

Harbinger was going to have a cardiac arrest. I dropped the shovel and walked around the side of the house. Harbinger was standing on the driveway looking up at the roof with that stupid, perplexed look of his. His hair was curly and he kept it pretty short. His round face was always sunburned. He was kinda overweight, too.

"You're not done yet?" he asked.

"Uh … I think you should see something."

"As a matter of fact, I don't have much time," he grumbled as he followed me around to the backyard.

I had never seen anybody as shocked as Harbinger was when he saw what I'd done. He was completely silent at first. And then he got really mad and started cussing at me. And then he was quiet again, holding his head in his hands and then he got mad again and threw his measuring tape at the ground.

"Bogart, I knew you were an idiot, but this is goddamn unbelievable!" Harbinger walked around to the other side of the hole and knelt down.

I was just standing still. "Harbinger, I—"

He stood up quickly and pointed at me. "No, no, no. Bogart. Don't talk, you listen! You've goddamn done enough, for chrissakes!"

"But—"

"What the hell were you thinking! You're supposed to be up there on the roof, laying those shingles, not digging up their septic tank! You just dug your own grave, Bogart. That's it. That's ... it. What am I supposed to tell Mr. Anderson, eh?"

"I don't know."

"Are you some kind of mental case, Bogart?"

"Hollis told me to."

"Huh?"

"I said—"

"Bogart, you're a real piece of work, you know that. If Hollis told you to jump off a bridge, would you do that too?"

I didn't know why grown-ups couldn't think of something better than the "jumping off the bridge" example of doing something without thinking. Talk about not thinking—the contradiction seemed pretty obvious to me. I didn't take the opportunity to point it out to Harbinger, though. I just shrugged and said, "No."

"And I don't believe for a millisecond that Hollis Mulwray told you to come down here and do this. Not for a microsecond," he repeated.

"Well—"

"Bogart!" he shouted. He picked up a shovel and threw it around a couple of times.

He told me (and the rest of the neighborhood, by the way) that I was going to have to pay for all the mess I'd made and the damage I'd done. I'd figured as much.

Finally, when Harbinger was totally out of breath and done grilling me, I asked him if I still had my job. It happened in a camera flash—I reckon asking about the job was a bad idea. He just lunged at me. He didn't see the shovel, the wooden handle of which rose to the occasion and hit him squarely in the face.

I know you shouldn't go around making assumptions, but I assumed right then that I had been fired. So I made my getaway while Harbinger clutched his bloody, bulbous nose. I ran to the front yard, grabbed by backpack off the front porch, and cut across the street and over a creek and into another subdivision before stopping to catch my breath.

I sat on one of those greenish electrical boxes—the kind that you think might randomly devour you in a fiery explosion of electricity at any minute. Trying not to think about what had just happened, I got to weighing the pros and cons of going to my last class of summer school—I mean, no student in the history of education ever learned anything useful on the last day of school. Eventually I made up my mind to go, because…what the hell? I just didn't want to go home and face Aunt Mel about getting fired.

Seven

Twin brothers Ricky and Owen were standing in front of the room bickering like school children, and it was really starting to annoy me. They had been at it for several minutes and it was obvious that Mr. Greenbaum wasn't paying enough attention to what was going on in the class, least of all to their history presentation. Not that I cared one way or another.

Mr. Greenbaum was a slouchy, squirrelly man, thin and wiry, real fidgety. He had all these irritating physical ticks that made it hard to take him very seriously. Jerking his head slightly to the left or squishing his nose sometimes or pursing his lips. Every now and then he sort of blinked his eyes several times really fast. Like when you go to the optometrist and they shoot that stupid air gun into your eyes. As if some doctor just did that to him or something. Obviously, Mr. Greenbaum was more of a distraction than a teacher. He was like a one-man show when he was standing in front of the class.

By far the most disgusting and the most annoying of all his ticks was how he always brushed his hair back with his hand. See, he was mostly bald on the dome, but what hair he did have was kinda greasy and combed straight back. So all day he rubbed his hand over the top of his head, from the front to the back, just to make sure his thinning hair was still thinning and his greasy hair was still greasy. He did this all the time—about a hundred times a day. His nickname was Greasepalm.

Greasepalm's pants were always crooked. It's hard not to notice when someone's back pockets are all off-kilter. Like, one pocket is on his hip and the other is right in the center of his ass. And that's how Greasepalm wore his pants. I don't know how he walked around like that.

Trying to forget about getting the ax from Mulwray Construction, I glanced around the room. The floors were a puke-green color, and I realized that most things in the school were the color of puke—the national color of learning. And plastered all over the walls were these stupid posters of flowers and mountains with inspirational quotes about determination and teamwork and the joy of life. I didn't get the purpose of those posters in the classroom; they were just distractions—like when you were at the dentist and you leaned back and looked at the ceiling and there were pictures of little chickadees taped up there to distract you from the drilling and filling going on in your mouth.

No matter how distracted I was, I still felt like shit, like a real dumb-ass loser for getting set up by Hollis, getting fired, and then on top of it all, having to pay Mulwray Construction for the damage to that septic tank.

I couldn't do anything right.

Greenbaum's final assignment had been to create a playable game incorporating something that had been studied during the summer. I thought it sounded like something that Mr. Greenbaum came up with at two in the morning after a couple of drinks, but what the hell, he was the teacher and we were the students. So we were supposed to trust that Greasepalm knew what he was doing.

To his credit, although he was arguably the worst history teacher in the known universe, he could work the hell out of a Sudoku puzzle. Which is what he was doing during the Miller twins' little game-show disaster. If the class didn't care about what Ricky and Owen had to say before they started quarreling, they certainly didn't give a damn about it during the argument. Most of the students had subtracted themselves from the learning equation a long time ago, and I was no exception. The bell rang. It was time to go home and tell Aunt Mel that I'd been fired from my job. The very thought terrified me.

Greenbaum stood up from behind his monstrous oak desk and pushed his grade book over the sudoku puzzle. (From what I saw, it was his pencil eraser that was doing most of the work.) As if we didn't know what he had been doing? He puffed out his chest to show he was the boss. He tugged at the sides of his pants just to make sure they looked stupid and brushed down his tie. Then he rubbed his hand over his head. Yep, still greasy.

"Great job. Give the Millers a hand…" he said demonstratively. He always did that. One or two folks clapped half-heartedly.

"You suck," someone said.

"Come on, you guys," moaned Greenbaum. "And girls," he continued, as he squished his nose and jerked his head a little.

You know that look folks give you when you're saying something to them, but they're really waiting for you to finish talking so they can say something to someone else? They keep, sort of, leaning in that other person's direction and their head starts turning, but their eyes stay looking at you as if only their head was magnetized or something? That's the look Mr. Greenbaum was giving the class as he gravitated toward his sudoku puzzle.

I gathered my belongings, wrapping the rubber band

tightly around my deck of playing cards. I had been practicing shuffling the deck of cards with one hand. The one hand that I kept below the desk. The one hand that nobody could see. There were perks to having a hobby that you can carry in the palm of your hand and play almost anywhere you go.

Even if that hobby gets you into trouble.

I made my way to the front of the room and toward the door, and then Greasepalm turned on me. "How're your moving plans?" he asked. "I hear that there aren't too many places with vacancies. That rent is sky high."

In nearly any conceivable scenario, walking by a teacher's desk was always a risky endeavor. If the hallway was the DMZ, the few feet in front of the teacher's desk were like that last ten yards leading up to the barbed wire bridge that's always in World War II or Vietnam movies and that was always the most guarded and dangerous. That was the few feet in front of the teacher's desk.

"Fine, Mr. Greenbaum." I waited a moment, catching a glimpse at Greasepalm eyeballing his puzzle. I took a step toward the door and just as I did, he asked me another question. I responded with "all right, well…you too," in sort of a good-bye way. I was hoping to throw him off. I know that sounds like something a little kid would do, deliberately saying the wrong thing to a simple question, but I didn't feel like talking just then.

Greasepalm was not thrown off, and he kept talking. "I remember when Hurricane Norman came through in '81," he said. "I think it was '81. I think maybe it was '82. Well, that doesn't make sense because I was...let's see here..." I thought, why the hell did he need me to talk to himself? Greenbaum went on for a while. "Anyway, the point is, it was a real beast, ripped everything to shreds."

Thanks a lot, I thought, real insightful—imagine that, a hurricane ripping everything to shreds. They must pay you a lot, Mr. Greasepalm. Seeing as how brilliant you are, you should be put in one of those think tanks where really brilliant folks just think and make really astute observations, like, "the hurricane ripped everything to shreds." Introducing—de facto brain-trust superstar, Mr. Kenneth Greasepalm!

I didn't say any of that stuff.

I could feel the outside magnetizing and my body start to gravitate toward the door. My eyes remained on Greenbaum as my head and my hips began shifting to the right. "I've gotta get home, Mr. Greenbaum, so..." I trailed off, trying not to make it too obvious that I just didn't care what he had to say. I thought it best to be discreet.

Greenbaum looked me up and down, noticing my deck of cards, which I was again shuffling with one hand.

"You a gambling man?" he asked, as if he had just tied up his horse or something.

"I dunno. Depends," I replied.

"Well then," he said, "good luck with moving out because with the way the rental market is right now, you're going to need it, I think."

"Thanks," I said as I turned away. I wasn't thanking Greasepalm for his insight, but for reminding me of something very, very important—something that just might save my ass now that I was fired.

Eight

I knew that when I got home, Aunt Mel was going to be upset and disappointed in me. I hoped that she wouldn't be there, but the odds of that were pretty slim because she usually only left the trailer once, or maybe twice, a week to get groceries or her paycheck or go to church. She never picked me up from work or school. But that was okay because I knew it wasn't because she didn't want to. She just really didn't have the energy. On account of her being partially crippled and so depressed and sleepy all the time.

And walking or taking the bus wasn't so bad, 'cause Aunt Mel's car smelled like puke and rotting water after it got flooded in Hurricane Leland. The water, which was pretty polluted to begin with, had settled into the upholstery. It was actually a miracle that the car still worked. Aunt Mel said it was "because it was made in America." Even though she believed that the United States government was out to get her, she was still proud to be an American. (Aunt Mel was against all institutions, except church.) I could hardly stand riding in her car, because the inside really did smell pretty awful and the windows didn't roll down because the mechanics got rusted and ruined and stuck in the *up* position. The air conditioner didn't work either, so it was really just like driving around in a rank hotbox.

There were lots of folks who'd lost cars and stuff in the hurricane, so I wasn't the only one walking. You saw people all around town, walking in groups of four or five or even families of ten sometimes. Those were the unlucky ones, without a car or money for the bus or to pay Jackson for a ride. Some were pretty old too. And those were the really unlucky ones.

Walking toward Route 5, I went past a police officer pulling someone over. I wondered if that guy steering his sedan to the shoulder was ashamed. It'd mortify me if I ever got pulled over by a cop on the side of the road. It's not the same as doing something stupid in front of one or two people. On the side of the road, it's doing something embarrassing in front of an endless amount of folks driving past thinking that you're a total sucker. And there was a lot of traffic on the way from the school to the trailer park.

That is, until Route 5.

Hardly anybody drove along that road. Most folks were afraid to, because kids threw or shot things at the cars. Kids threw things because they were bored silly or they were just cruel and stupid. Maybe a little bit of all three.

About three months ago, a guy got shot with a rifle. Right through the front window. Killed him, too. It caused quite a hubbub for a few days, then everyone forgot or didn't care. They never found the person who shot him. A little while after that, someone threw a baseball into someone's window and it caused such a distraction that he wrecked his car into a palm tree and then into a sewage ditch. That person didn't die, he only got paralyzed from the waist down. Sucks to be that guy. I think I'd rather die than have to cruise around in one of those electronic wheel chairs. That's just me, though; I'm sure there are lots of folks who would rather live like that.

The trailer park wasn't legally or officially called the Straits, but that's how everyone referred to it. At least, everyone who lived there. Folks who didn't live there called it dangerous or a nuisance. The official name of the trailer park was Florida Mid-Atlantic Regional FEMA Housing Park. But who was gonna take the time to say all that? No matter what folks called it, everyone knew exactly what they are referring to—errant baseballs and deadly bullets.

The park had only been there for about nine months. Just since Hurricane Leland flooded and destroyed a bunch of houses. Leland left all these folks with no place to go and no place to live, so the government brought in these trailers for them to live in until they found new apartments or a new houses. It was only supposed to be temporary, but that was like, nine months ago and nine months sure didn't feel very temporary to me.

Last May, the Federal Emergency Management Agency announced that on September 1st everyone had to begin moving out of the Straits to some other new home— 'cause they needed the trailers for other displaced folks. I understood that others needed the trailers, but what the hell were we supposed to do? Sounded like robbing Peter to pay Paul, if you ask me.

As I walked along Route 5, I thought about how Aunt Mel and I only had a few days left to get enough money to move into an apartment. It's why I had been working so hard all goddamn summer long. Because if the deadline came and went without a new apartment, who knew what was going to happen to Aunt Mel and me. We'd probably have to go live in an alley or an abandoned middle school gymnasium somewhere and what would my mom have thought if I let that happen?

Between the both of us, we'd saved up a lot of money, but definitely not enough to move into our own apartment.

Maybe if apartments and houses weren't so damn expensive. But ever since Hurricane Leland destroyed so many places to live, a lot of folks had to find new homes and so rents skyrocketed, practically double in price from what they were before the storm. It got me thinking that our country wasn't founded on liberty and freedom so much as on supply and demand. And I didn't entirely blame the folks who were charging so much, because I reckon they should be free to charge whatever the hell they want. I blame the government 'cause their job was to govern, and bringing in trailers and then taking them away wasn't governing. That's gross misconduct, if you ask me, and whoever made that decision should be fired. Maybe Aunt Mel was onto something with her acute paranoia, after all.

When we all got the news about being forced to move out of the Straits, everyone was were pretty much up in arms about it. But we weren't smart or rich enough to do anything about it. "I don't like this any more than you do, Jim," Aunt Mel had said optimistically, "but seeing as we are all that either of us have, we gotta make it work." We were in the checkout line at the grocery store. It was a Sunday afternoon and the place was packed.

"I remember after your sister was born, when your dad up and left, Jim." She paused and thought long and hard for a second or two, and then said, "What a shitbag!" Aunt Mel never liked my old man, but she didn't have to tell that to the little kids in the candy aisle.

"Your mom was in a real fix, Jim, what with two little

kids and no money and no job!" Aunt Mel leaned heavily on her walking cane. "Pssshhh, but I helped her out, Jim, cause that's what you do. In this world, you gotta help each other out."

"I know," I said. "You've told me that a thousand times."

Ignoring me, Aunt Mel continued. "And let me just tell you, after she got into that assistance program and then met mister what's-his-face and got that job at the Academy, and after she was able to rent her own house and pay her own bills, Jim, you know what she said to me?" Aunt Mel paused to catch her breath. But it was kind of a long pause.

"Do you want me to ans—?"

"She said that she was proud of *me*, Jim. That was the first time in my life that anybody had ever said that they were proud of me! The first time, at fifty..." she trailed off. "At my age. It meant more than anything to hear her say that, and trust me, I didn't expect her to and she didn't have to."

She stared at me for another long time, letting the information sink into my brain. Then she waved her finger and said, "I know you feel bad about what happened to your mom and sister. I do too. They're gone, Jim, but you can still honor them by doing the right thing!" I thought about that as she went on and on about something off the subject (I think a magazine headline had caught her eye or something). When she said that stuff about the right thing, I saw the cashier lady nodding her head, like she was in the conversation or something.

By the time we paid for our groceries and made it out to the stinky-shit car, Aunt Mel had firmly established and reiterated several times, in different ways, how I needed to be the man that my shitbag dad never was. How I needed to make my mom and sister proud by making enough money over the summer that we could move out, into our very own apartment.

On the drive back home, she explained to me again, for the thousandth time, why *she* couldn't work properly—on account of the thing with her leg. Her prognosis was different every time. I didn't believe she had anything clinically wrong with her leg, but I also didn't have the heart to confront her about it. I thought she was just depressed, which made her not want to go anywhere or do anything. Somehow she must have convinced herself that she had contracted a leg problem just so she had an outward excuse to stay in and sulk.

But I didn't hold it against Aunt Mel for basically throwing *all* the responsibility onto me, making me the one who'd have to save us from living out of a cardboard box (if it came to that). Because I wanted to save us. I needed to do something right for once.

Nine

I arrived at the Straits and walked up "A" Road to the 300s. I lived in the 300s. I saw Mr. Williams watering his lawn. By lawn, I mean the little patch of ground surrounding his trailer that didn't even belong to him. I don't know why he even cared. I looked at each tinny, white trailer after tinny, white trailer. Every time I went through the park, it still struck me how sterile and depressing it all was.

When we first got here, the government promised us a post office, a convenience store, and a playground. Those would have made life a little more bearable. But they didn't do any of those things because of liabilities and funding shortages or some pure bullshit. The only thing they gave us was a laundry facility that was completely overpriced.

The Straits was set up in an abandoned fairgrounds on the southern edge of Ambricourt. It was intended to be organized like a grid: each dusty gravel road was a letter of the alphabet, and each trailer was numbered. And the trailers were all the same, indistinguishable from one another. You could get lost in there pretty easily, and I had on several occasions.

I got home and swung the trailer door open, coming face to face with Aunt Mel, who was just on her way out the door. She was going to take a Tupperware container of cookies to the neighbors across the way.

"Still no luck?" I asked, as I squeezed past her and opened the refrigerator door. I was trying to act like it was just another normal day.

Aunt Mel had gray hair and, like most middle-aged women, had it cut short and round. From a distance it looked like a gray motorcycle helmet. And her hair never moved. She could pop her head out the sunroof of a moving car and it wouldn't budge.

She always wore black tights that were pretty gross, and nasty old flannel shirts that were *enormous*. More like muu-muus than shirts, really. They hung down to her knees. It was a disastrous ensemble, but she pulled it off as well as anyone could. And anyway, she stayed inside most of the time so it didn't really matter what she looked like, I reckon.

"Do you mind taking them over there for me, now that you're home?"

The distant trailer across the field was a complete mystery. First of all, it was different from all the rest—it was a lot dumpier and it was kind of rusty and sagged to one side. And it was stuck a few hundred feet away from the rest of the park, near the tree line. It was just off by itself for no apparent reason; it wasn't one of the tainted ones that had been removed because of the formaldehyde fumes, either. There wasn't even a gravel road leading up to it. And it didn't even have a proper number.

The big mystery was that there were never any cars parked around the trailer, and nobody had ever seen the occupants coming or going in all the months that we had been living in the Straits.

Not once.

Since we were on the corner, we had a pretty good view of the distant trailer from our living room window. Aunt Mel had become obsessed with seeing who lived there. When she wasn't working or napping with the television on, she'd be looking out the window, alert, her eyes barely blinking. (Aunt Mel knew how to be unproductive better than anyone.)

At first, I thought it was actually a pretty fun idea. Trying to see the neighbors by luring them out with fresh baked goods left on their doorstep. But recently, considering how money was tight and we were getting down to the wire with the deadline and all, I thought we should be saving our resources and not baking handouts for the enigmatic neighbors that didn't matter anyhow.

And there was one fatal flaw in the plan. Aunt Mel's special cookies tasted like shit. They were nasty. I'd never told her so 'cause she was really proud of her secret recipe, which had been "passed down through the generations." Not that it seemed to make a difference. Aunt Mel would put the cookies out there on their doorstep and then the next day, the plastic container would be empty. So even though nobody ever saw who it was, somebody was eating the cookies.

I dropped off the container on the front step of the trailer and ran back. I didn't like hanging around over there because, honestly, the place kind of gave me the creeps.

From the front door, Aunt Mel watched me make the round trip. "I decided to buy the expensive ingredients. All name brands," she said, sitting down heavily on the sofa. I sat down next to her.

"Terrific," I said, sarcastically.

"Don't worry, Jim," she said. "I left a few for you."

"Even better."

"By the way, how was the last day of summer school? And work?"

"Fine and fine."

"Carla from next door was telling me that they found a place over in Calumet City for a reasonable price."

"That's 'cause Calumet's lame," I said without thinking.

"It's better than the Straits," she started. I watched her pick up a yellow rope and deftly knot it.

If I didn't act quickly, I knew that Aunt Mel would be talking about god knows what for god knows how long. She was always complaining about being mistreated this way or that way, and it often had to do with immigrants. I mean, I loved her because she was family, but all the speculation and griping could really get irritating. I reckon she did have a lot to complain about. For one thing, she lost all she had in Hurricane Leland—at least when you're as young as me, you didn't have much to lose. I mean, my mom and my sister were killed, but anyway, I didn't lose anything else that mattered. For goodness sake, Mel lost her collection of Christmas ornaments and her vintage teacups and all her furniture and her poor stuffed poodle. I remember this one dramatic episode where she was crying hysterically. She said that her poodle, Flike, was probably the only dog in Ambricourt that died twice. Flike died of old age, and then Flike drowned in the flood. Poor Flike, but I didn't think animals should be stuffed and kept around. It was weird.

"Y'know, Jim," Aunt Mel said. "You've done a really good job this summer. You've worked so hard."

"Thanks," I said. "You've worked pretty hard, too." That was only half true—by nature, Aunt Mel's job didn't require her to work hard. A dog toy manufacturer had hired her to tie dog toys because she could do it in a sitting position. You know those dog toys with the long yellow ropes and the plastic thing on the end that you throw? Her job was to tie the plastic thing to the long yellow rope. Somebody had to do it, right? She got money for each one that she tied. It wasn't much, but it was something.

"By this time next week, we'll be in a real apartment!" she was saying. "Even if Calumet is lame, it's a real roof over our heads. Which is better than nothing. The Vargas family over on F Avenue won't have enough money to move, because Mr. Vargas is an alcoholic, you know. So god knows what they're going to do. Poor Evelyn. She said that she might have to go stay in a shelter. Can you imagine? A shelter!"

"Yeah." Boy, she couldn't have laid it on thicker if she knew I'd been fired.

"Oh, Kathy called," she added.

"She did? When?" I asked.

"Yesterday. I forgot to tell you."

"What did she want?"

"Something about a party on Friday. But I don't like the sound of that."

I went into my bedroom and closed the door behind me. I needed a little privacy—there weren't many things more uncomfortable than having a conversation with a girl like Kathy in front of your Aunt Mel.

I called Kathy's cell phone a couple of times, but she didn't answer, so I called her house phone. Mr. Montgomery picked up.

"Is Kathy there? This is Jim."

"Hey, Jim. It's Mr. Montgomery."

"Hey," I said.

He sorta chuckled to himself. "I didn't hear the phone ringing because of the music. I was playing it a little too loud."

"Yeah. The piano?" I didn't know why I asked that as if I didn't know—Mr. Montgomery played the piano pretty well, but he didn't know how to relate to folks. He was a pretty strange guy and his awkwardness was contagious. Just talking to him or being in his presence made me feel uncomfortable and self-conscious.

"Well, you want to talk to Kathy?"

"Yeah, is she around?"

"Just a sec," he said. I heard him yell Kathy's name a couple of times, and then he got back on. "Oh, you know what, Jim, she actually left. I forgot. She went to the mall. But she should have her cell phone. Try that."

"I will. Thanks," I said, and hung up the phone.

Ten

The sun had gone down long before I'd gotten in touch with Kathy and agreed to meet at the Walking Jay. When I arrived, she was alone in her favorite booth.

I pushed the glass door open with my elbow because I didn't want to touch the door. I know that sounds funny—hanging out in a place where you avoid touching the front door, but there were some real strange loons that stopped by and trust me, you didn't want to get any of that loon stuff on your hands.

The Walking Jay was built in the mid-eighties on a slight bluff overlooking the freeway. Eventually it became popular with all the high school kids. For whatever reason, it was *the* hangout. Over the years though the place had gotten pretty run down, but the teenagers just kept going. The lights on the sign out front didn't even work. Sometimes they flickered, but that's about all. But to the Walking Jay's credit, through every hurricane that stormed in, it never once got flooded or seriously damaged. Tacky was durable.

Everyone gathered at the Walking Jay after football games or late on a Saturday night or Sunday morning for a quick pick-me-up after several too many drinks, or after a devastating break-up, or after school to procrastinate doing homework or something. The place was open twenty-four hours and even at the most obscene time of night, the Walking Jay never discriminated between those who should be there—adults—and those of us who shouldn't be there—teenagers with nothing to do. At least, teenagers shouldn't have been there as far as most adults were concerned, but business is business and money is money. A teenager's money is as good as any geezer's; that's what Roy said, and he was a geezer. He owned the place. 'Course, Roy was a bit blind, a bit senile, and totally crazy, but what did we care so long as we had a hangout.

I slid into the booth across from Kathy. I really like booths—it's the only seat that's kinda fun to sit down in and get up from, what with all of the sliding involved.

"About time," she kidded.

I smiled. "It's been a long day."

"Ahh," she said. "Harbinger working you too much?"

I swallowed hard and pulled out a napkin and folded it in no particular way. "Not really," I said. I didn't want to lie to her, but I didn't want her to know the truth, either. See, Kathy had a thing about being honest. Not that that was a bad thing necessarily, but to her, there were no exceptions to the rule of always telling the truth. I think it had something to do with how her dad had lied about how her mom was doing healthwise until it was too late. Understandably, that had an impact, and Kathy was always careful to tell the truth in every situation no matter the consequences. And sometimes, there were consequences. For everyone.

Kathy was in my grade at Ambricourt Academy and she was pretty hot (and popular) for being smart, too—she was the student that teachers always called on after several volunteers gave the wrong answer. So what were the chances that someone like *me* would hook up with someone like Kathy Montgomery? About the same odds as flopping a royal flush.

There was a half-eaten club sandwich in front of her. She had pushed the plate into the middle of the table.

"How was Galveston?" I asked, changing the subject. Kathy had gone to Galveston for a few days to visit family.

"Kind of boring, actually. It was good to see my cousins, but they just sit around and, like, stare at each other. I'm glad to be back."

"What've you been doing since you got home?"

"Nothing, really," she said. "We had a late birthday lunch for Mr. Mulwray at their clubhouse. That place is *so* nice."

"Was Hollis behaving himself?" I asked.

She smiled in a way that made me feel a little sick. "Yeah," she said. "Y'know, Jim, he's not as bad as you think he is. I know he can be a little … juvenile sometimes, but I don't think that's any reason why you two should hate each other."

"He doesn't hate me cause he's juvenile," I explained. "He hates me because I'm better than him at cards and because he thinks I'm white trash."

"That's ridiculous," she said.

"That's the truth and you, for one, should know."

Kathy was always sticking up for Hollis. Their families had been friends for a long time. And Kathy and Hollis had known each other practically their entire lives. And I think she felt loyalty to him because the Mulwrays had helped her dad out after her mother passed away from cervical cancer or something like that.

"Come on, Jim. You're just still hanging on to what happened at the Academy. That was so long ago. Besides, it was your word against his, for goodness sake. And that's what you get for gambling in the first place."

"It was in the newspaper, Kathy, it was a big deal. You'd still be hanging on to it if it happened to you."

"*That* would never happen to me, Jim."

"I forgot, you're perfect, aren't you?"

"That's not what I meant," she replied. "What's with you tonight? You're so touchy."

I decided to let it go, which is what I had to do every time it came up because there was just no changing her mind about it. Unless there was hard proof of Hollis' involvement in our gambling ring, she just was going to give him the benefit of the doubt.

"I'm just fired. I mean, tired—that's all," I said.

Eleven

Kathy had brown hair and a cute face. She took real good care of her skin and it showed. It was olive-colored and flawless, almost radiant in a way. The first time I remember seeing Kathy, I think, was at a basketball game. I was in seventh grade—my first year at the Academy. I was at the game because my mom had monitor duty (which meant that my younger sister, Martha, and I had to tag along too). Martha and I were in line at the concession stand. I hated concession stands because they were always swarming with kids chewing huge pieces of gum. I was in a foul mood because there was this little two-year-old staring at me. What're you looking at? I thought. You're the one with shit running down your chin.

"What do you want?" I asked Martha, without taking my eyes off that two-year-old.

"Yogurt." She was still a little kid so she didn't know that they didn't sell yogurt at school sporting events.

"I don't think they have yogurt, Martha. Pick something else." I looked down at that two-year-old without moving my head or any muscle in my body, just my eyes. He was still staring at me. I suddenly glared right at him and made a scary face. The kid ran off crying. I didn't mean to frighten him that bad, I just wanted him to stop staring at me.

"Uh huh," I heard Martha say.

"Do you wanna bet? This isn't a grocery—"

Kathy was standing behind us, eavesdropping. She tapped me on the shoulder and said, "Look." She pointed. I saw, on the menu board, that they did sell those little cups of yogurt. "Ah, damn," I said.

"See," Martha started, "and you shouldn't curse cause Mom said so."

Kathy was short and had on these tortoiseshell glasses.

I got to the front of the line and bought Martha a strawberry yogurt, and she took it and ran off before I could give her a spoon. I ordered some nachos and a coke, like you were supposed to do at a concession stand. I was doctoring up my nachos with some pepper and salt and that kinda stuff and Kathy came over.

"What'd you do to that kid?" she asked. "That kid who ran off crying?"

"Nothing." Yeah, I thought, deny everything.

"Well, you must've done something."

"You wanna bet?" I challenged her.

We were standing in front of the little napkin dispenser, the kind that never works right. Of course, the napkins were jammed stuck. I smiled at Kathy and then gave that drawer a serious pull and practically threw out my shoulder in the process. When I yanked it, that goddamn dispenser came flying out and the napkins went everywhere. I dropped the drawer and it clanged, clanged, clanged against the tile floor. Everyone turned and looked, and it was the most embarrassing thing in the world. Kathy laughed and bent down to start picking up the napkins. I kneeled down and started picking them up with her, careful not to touch that disgusting floor. "Thanks," I said.

"Wasn't that your sister you were with?"

"Yeah."

"Does she play cards with you?"

"Huh?" I asked.

"I've seen you with that deck of cards. Everyone has."

"Why, do you like to play?"

"Not really," she said.

"Yeah." I tried to be macho as I crunched down authoritatively on my nacho. "It's not for everyone."

"My mom taught me that gambling is wrong," she offered.

"Oh, yeah," I said. "Well, that's her opinion."

Kathy nodded. "Still," she said, "most of the games seem based on perception."

We stood there for a moment. I ate another nacho. Kathy asked how I liked school.

"Not much."

She glanced around the gym lobby.

"Where'd you move here from?" I asked.

"Texas."

"That's cool. I think I have family in Texas or something." I didn't know anyone in Texas, but it seemed like something you say.

We stood there for a moment, both kinda feeling awkward.

"So what's your sister's name?" she asked.

"Martha. I was supposed to be keeping my eye on her, but that's more difficult than it sounds. She's always running off and I'm always losing her." I could see Martha on the other side of the lobby; she was standing around a group of boys, eating her yogurt with her little tiny fingers. "But she's cool most of the time."

"How old is she?"

"Nine."

We finished picking up all the napkins and stood up.

"You wanna nacho?"

"No thanks," she said. "I have yogurt."

"Yogurt, huh? I hate opening up those foil lids, y'know,

because the yogurt just explodes all over the place and it always gets on my shirt. It's disgusting."

"Disgusting?"

"Like, see that guy over there? He's disgusting." I was pointing at Hollis Mulwray who, along with several of his friends, was wetting clumps of toilet paper at the water fountain and throwing them against the ceiling.

"Who, Hollis?"

"He *is* the one throwing toilet paper at the ceiling, isn't he?"

"He's my date to the dance this weekend," she acknowledged sheepishly.

"What bet did you lose?" I joked. She didn't laugh.

A clump of toilet paper fell off the ceiling and landed with a squash on the floor. Hollis and his friends laughed pretty hard at that. For some reason or another.

"Going out with an upperclassman, eh?"

"Not really. I dunno. Our families know each other." Then after a few more awkward seconds of her glancing around the lobby and me chuckling at things that just weren't that funny, she asked, "How come you're so anti-social?"

"I get around."

She smirked. "With who?"

"Russ," I said. The truth was that she was making a pretty good point. "And Charlie…sometimes." It was true, I did keep to myself. But just 'cause I wanted to be left alone didn't mean I was doing crazy experiments in my garage or something. I just didn't know how to go about hobnob-bing between classes. And making friends is a process that takes years. That's what I told myself, anyway.

In any event, I thought it best to change the subject. "My mom's one of the high school English teachers."

"I know."

"Yeah. What about your parents?"

"My dad's just started as a music teacher at the Ambri-court Community College and he's going to give piano lessons at the house."

"I bet all that noise just *kills* your mom!"

She stopped smiling. "Actually, she died last year," she mumbled.

"Oh, damn. Sorry."

"It's okay," she replied softly. "I'll see you later. Well, enjoy your nachos."

"Yeah," I said pathetically. "Enjoy the dance." I knew that was an idiotic thing to say, but it was all I could think of.

She turned and walked away, joining a group of girls by the bathrooms. I watched them talking in the corner as I polished off my nachos. And then Hollis and his friends joined them and then they all went outside. And then I went to find Martha.

As I wandered around the lobby and the gym and under the bleachers and outside the front doors, I thought about that little kid I scared and the napkin incident. And then I thought about Kathy. And the more I thought about her, the more I liked her. The more I liked her, the more I thought about her.

I found Martha and scolded her for running off. She was supposed to stay where I could see her. She was always running off, no matter what I told her. She never listened and I always had to go track her down. And I found her in the gymnasium, on the stage, behind the curtain (nobody was supposed to be up there). She was rolling around on one of those cushioned blue mats that gymnasts use for practice. There were actually a bunch of mats rolled up and unfurled and just sorta thrown on the stage. A bunch of kids, Martha's age mostly, were having a good time playing on them. It looked ridiculous, all those kids, like fifteen at least, playing on those mat things. After I watched for a few minutes, I joined them and it was pretty fun. 'Course, I was twice as big as all the other kids, but they didn't care. They thought I was cool and for the rest of the time that I wrestled and tossed those kids around on those goddamn mats, I was cool.

Twelve

Kathy was looking out the window, or at her reflection in the window. I couldn't tell.

"What are you doing tonight?" I asked her.

She looked at me. "I dunno for sure yet," she said in a way that indicated that she definitely did know but didn't want to say. "What are you doing?"

"Nothing," I said glumly. I picked up her club sandwich and peeled off the top piece of bread to see if she had put that Dijon mustard on there. I didn't like Dijon mustard.

"I put Dijon mustard on it."

"I see."

"I saw Mel down at the grocery store earlier today. Looked like she was going to do some serious baking."

"Yeah," I mumbled, not at all wanting to talk about Aunt Mel's baking habits.

I looked up as Nancy Davis entered. She was one of Kathy's older friends, one of those girls who wants adults to think she's nice but everyone her age knows she's naughty. She was in Hollis' class. Following her was skanky Vera Danner that Hollis got with, and her twin brother, Jesse. What a duo. Jesse wore glasses and talked with a severely distracting lisp. Fortunately, someone else did most of the talking for him. And like I said, Vera was the type of girl who always had a boyfriend, sometimes more than one at the same time. How could anybody make out with Vera without thinking about Jesse? Or vice versa for that matter. And who wants to think of a girl's brother when you're making out, especially with a lisping one like Jesse—"kith me, baby."

Vera was talking on her cell phone. Jesse went to the refrigerators in the back and got a soda.

I glanced at Nancy, who was greeting Kathy by talking about their clothes or a swimsuit.

Nancy and Kathy in swimsuits, I thought.

And then Hollis strolled in. "Look who it is—Mr. Summer School," he said. He flirtatiously threw his arm around Kathy, who laughed and pushed it off. "How's work going?" he asked me, as if he didn't know.

"Fine," I said. I didn't want to talk about getting fired.

Kathy graciously tolerated Hollis' constant advances and come-ons. I think she found something cool about being associated with him—even if he was a complete phony. She'd gone to Homecoming with him and one or two school dances, but that was all I knew. I'm sure their parents thought it was just cute. To my knowledge, though, she'd never fooled around with him. Not for lack of his trying.

I'd avoided most extracurricular school functions when I was at the Academy, because someone had to take advantage of the option to stay home and do nothing.

Jesse paid for his soda and stood next to Vera.

Everyone was in a conversation except for me. I just sat there trying not to look as uncomfortable as I felt.

Hollis whispered something to Jesse and they both started laughing. Hollis slapped Jesse on the arm. It was obvious that whatever they were laughing at had something to do with me. Kathy shot him a glance and he responded by shrugging his shoulders and then slapping Jesse on the arm. Jesse agreed with Hollis' shoulder shrugging, I reckon, because he sort of smiled and chortled. I noted that Hollis and Jesse were employing a communication technique called "primitive," used mostly used in the jungles of South America or Malaysia by gorillas and like-minded knuckle-draggers.

Vera hung up her phone and stepped forward. "So, are we going to leave or what?"

Kathy slid out of the booth and stood next to Nancy. "Do you want to go, Jim?" she asked politely.

"Where to?"

"A movie. They reopened the theater down on Carver Street." During the last hurricane, Carver Street had flooded pretty badly. There were lots of shops and such on Carver Street, so obviously they'd worked pretty diligently to get the place shoppable again.

Hollis, Jesse, and Vera gave Kathy a sincere look of disapproval. Vera said, "I don't think there's enough room in the car, Kathy."

Nancy and Vera didn't like me. I never really understood why, and frankly, never really cared.

"No thanks," I said. "Maybe another night."

"You're welcome," Hollis snapped as he turned and headed for the door. Jesse and Vera followed him.

Kathy walked out last. On purpose, of course, because she wanted to say something to me in private.

"Are you sure you don't want to go?"

"I don't think so," I said. "I don't want to be the sixth wheel. Besides, you and Jesse need some alone-time."

Kathy grimaced. "Thath's dithguthting."

I couldn't help laughing.

"I didn't think you'd want to, but I thought I'd ask," she added. "It's just that we made plans before you called me today…"

I interrupted her. "It's okay. Seriously. Thanks for asking."

She started toward the door, but hesitated. "Are you going to the Wilmots'?"

The party that nobody wanted me to attend, as Hollis had so confidently assured me earlier. "Why would I?" I asked.

"For fun," she said with a mirthless smile.

I thought about it for a second. "It's not like I'm friends with anyone there anymore."

"Who cares?"

"Me," I looked down at her club sandwich again.

Kathy was quiet again. A car honked and she looked out the window. Hollis flashed his sports-car lights. "Well, maybe *I* want you there."

Deep down I wanted to go to the Wilmots'. "When is it?" I asked, deliberately prolonging the conversation.

"This Friday."

"What about Hollis?"

"What about him? He's just going to get drunk, come on to me, then make a fool out of himself and end up at the Walking Jay with everyone else," she said with a little smile and a touch on my arm. And then she was out the door.

I thought, was she just flirting with me?

A few moments passed before I realized I was alone in the booth. Kathy was gone and Hollis was gone and Nancy, Jesse, and Vera were gone. I glanced out the window to see Mathers trying to direct traffic again—he was waving his arms, gesturing each automobile into its place next to the station.

As the resident weirdo of the Walking Jay, Mathers dressed in dirty old clothes that were thoroughly torn and frayed. He was always at the Walking Jay. For all anyone knew, he lived in a box out back. I always wanted to ask him where he spent the night, but I didn't want to offend him. I reckon I could've followed him home, but I didn't care that much.

He'd started showing up at the Walking Jay a few months ago and ever since then he was constantly bothering the hell out of everybody, indiscriminately intruding on any conversation he overheard. And he just talked and talked (that is, when he wasn't doing something crazy like directing traffic in the parking lot) and said "yep" a lot. He always brought up the same three or four subjects, too—funny stories involving human interaction with reptiles, Leonardo da Vinci, physics (a lot about the space-time continuum), and lastly, the meaning of life. Mathers was good at manipulating any conversation back to those few subjects. Once, I overheard him jump from a piece of burnt toast to the wave-particle duality and then to the Vitruvian Man and then to something in the news about someone who got caught trying to steal a python from the zoo in a metal trash can. Mathers did all this in a single breath. I don't think Roy cared about Mathers all that much, given that Roy was kinda crazy himself.

Mathers claimed to have a son or something, but nobody ever took that seriously because nobody ever saw him. And he also claimed to have lived in every state in the union. Yeah, right.

His face looked like a baseball mitt, due to how used and worn it was. His chain-smoking didn't help. And he'd snap off the filters and plug the paper and tobacco into a little piece of straw that he carried with him in his shirt pocket. He claimed to be in his sixties, but there was really no way in hell he was a day younger than eighty.

I took what was left of Kathy's sandwich and wrapped it in a napkin. I enjoyed my slide out of the booth and went to the door, opening it with my elbow again.

When Mathers saw me exiting the Jay, he hurried over and asked if I had any change.

"No," I said. "But you want a club sandwich?"

"Sure," he replied.

I handed him the napkin with the sandwich, and after giving it a cursory once-over he asked, "It doesn't have Dijon, does it?"

"You don't have a sense of smell so you can't taste, remember?" I didn't mind old Mathers that much. In fact, I kinda liked him. I knew he was just lonely, so I let him talk to me whenever he wanted because if I were as old and as alone as he seemed to be, I'd like someone to talk to as well. And besides, some of the things he said were funny and he was pretty nice guy for having so many missing teeth.

Mathers smiled his ugly smile. "Oh, yeah. That's right." He took a bite of the sandwich. "Were those your buddies with you, Jim?"

"Buddies? Not really."

"That one boy drives a nice car."

"Hollis."

"I tried to give him directions. He wouldn't listen."

"I wouldn't think so." I watched Mathers take another bite of the sandwich. He wiped his face with his hand. "Why were you directing traffic?"

He stuffed the rest of the sandwich into his mouth and smiled. "Just 'cause," he said. He wiped his mouth like a kid and looked off into the hazy, dark distance beyond the lights of the Walking Jay. Like he'd heard some call of the wild.

"Mathers, can I ask you a question?"

"Yep."

"Shouldn't you be at home or something?"

"Something?"

"Well, don't you have a house?"

"Sure," he said, again smiling that hideous smile of cavities and gingivitis. I felt bad for him—I thought he just needed someone to care for him. Someone to tell him that he mattered. Someone to remind him to floss.

"But it's more interesting here," he finished.

"I reckon you're right," I said, patting him on the back. "I'll see you later."

"Yep."

Thirteen

As I walked home, back through the Straits, I shuffled my cards and thought about what I had to do. See, when Mr. Greenbaum asked if I was a gambling man, it made me think of the conversation I'd had with Jackson. I thought about the floating gambling parlor again and decided that after Jackson got me into the game and I won his money back, I could stay and win enough money to help me and Aunt Mel move out of the trailer park. Sure, it wasn't the gold standard of failproof plans and if my mom were still alive, she'd beat me blue for even thinking about gambling with what little savings we had left, but desperate times called for desperate measures. It's not like

Harbinger was beating down my door to see me again, much less to give me my job back or write off how much it was going to cost to fix the septic tank.

The more I thought about gambling on Sycamore Street, the more anxious I felt. That's why I was shuffling my cards. It was a bit of a nervous habit, at least whenever my deck was handy, and it mostly was handy—I took that deck of cards with me everywhere I went just in case there was someone who wanted to play a few hands. It was a special deck. It was the only thing I had from my father and he's not around to give me anything else, so I had to be careful with it. Not that I was supposed to like my old man. He ran out on us after Martha was born. My mom didn't talk about him all that much. And that was okay because when she did talk about him, she got emotional and stuff which made me feel kinda hopeless. To me, my mom was the captain of the ship and no first mate wanted to see their captain crying into a bowl of Top Ramen. It just wasn't a boon for morale. Not the kind of image you want running through your mind during a crisis.

I never told my mom, but I thought about my dad sometimes and after she and Martha died, I kinda hoped that he'd come back for me. But he didn't even go to the funeral.

I went inside the trailer and found Aunt Mel standing in the living room. She was peeking out of the front blinds toward the trailer across the street.

"D'you see them?" I asked.

"Not yet. And I'm getting worried. There's only four days left until we have to leave." I didn't exactly think that was what she should be worried about, but what the hell. "Aren't you out late, Jim?" she continued, not diverting her calculated gaze.

"I dunno. Did you put more cookies over there?"

"Yeah. I doubled the batch."

Terrific, I thought, we're broke and you're doubling the batch. "Well, I'm going to bed. I'll see you tomorrow. Don't stay up too late."

She looked at me real quick. "I won't." And she returned her attention to the shadowless trailer across the street.

Thursday Morning, August 28

As the evaporation-condensation cycle of warm humid ocean air continues and the difference in air pressure between high and low altitudes is sustained, swirling winds of the tropical depression are recorded at 58 mph, thus elevating its status to tropical storm.

The National Hurricane Center in Miami, Florida, is notified.

Fourteen

When the *buzz, buzz, buzz* woke me up, I stumbled out of bed and fumbled with the clock in a sleepy fog. I couldn't find that damn switch. That *buzz, buzz, buzz* was bothering me so much, I yanked the plug out of the wall so I could go back to bed for another minute or two—I was still so sleepy. But then I slipped and fell on the way back into the bed, and that knocked the sleepy out of me. So I got dressed and brushed my teeth.

I had set the alarm for six in the morning because Aunt Mel expected me to leave for work at that time and I had to keep up proper impressions. Six in the morning was obscenely early to get up for a job I didn't have, let me tell you. Aunt Mel was asleep when I slowly made my way from my bedroom to the kitchen, the trailer floor creaking beneath each step.

I secretly and quietly took out the coffee can from below the sink. Inside was our entire summer savings in cash—it was in the coffee can because Aunt Mel was afraid of banks. Like I said, she was one of those folks who thought the economy was going to tank any minute and then the banks would be unable to pay anyone back for their investment or something. I don't know where Aunt Mel developed her Depression-era ideas. It's not like she read books or even the newspaper. We obviously didn't have the Internet.

So not only did I need money to gamble with on Sycamore Street with Jackson, but I needed money to pay Harbinger back for the damage I'd done to the septic tank. As much as I wanted to stick it to Harbinger and to Mulwray Construction company, I just couldn't. I didn't do a lot of things that I should, but I always paid my debts.

I wasn't a cheapskate.

I opened the coffee can and reached in and counted out half of what was in there—fifteen hundred dollars. Five hundred to pay Harbinger back and an additional thousand to gamble with. That seemed like a lot, but it really wasn't in gambling terms. I couldn't show up at the house with much less and still be considered with any amount of sincerity as a legitimate gambler. No one respects a player who sits down at the card table without at least ten times the ante. Otherwise you're just asking nicely to be bullied out of every pot.

The sun hadn't completely come up and there was still a cool breeze. It felt good against my face—it reminded me of the walks I used to take with my mom. I headed out of the Straits, past Everett the security guard, who was sleeping in his post. I saw his bootless, bare feet up on the table. That's the kind of job I wouldn't mind making a career of, I thought.

There weren't many cars out that early, but every now and then one sped past me. There weren't sidewalks, so I had to walk in the grass on the side of the road and since there was dew over everything, my shoes and socks got pretty wet. For the most part, it was all real quiet, except for the occasional car and the morning chorus of cicadas and croaking frogs. I saw some birds—a great blue heron, one or two pigeons and a barn swallow, and a family of mallard ducks. The only reason I knew anything about birds was because Kathy was into them and was some kind of member in the bird society.

When I got to Mulwray headquarters, Harbinger hadn't arrived. So I sat out on the curb until around nine, when he finally drove his big annoying truck into the lot. By that time the sun was heating things up pretty well. I was starting to sweat. I don't know if he was showing off or trying to be tough or something, but the asshole parked right in front of me, and I mean right in front of me. I was sitting on the curb facing this one particular parking space and he swung his truck into *that* spot when there were like a hundred parking spaces available for him to pull into. But he pulled into *that* one. So the goddamn grill to the truck came to a halt right in front of my face, inches from my nose. That's the kind of person Harbinger was—he'd park in the most conspicuous parking space of them all.

I stood up, almost tripping as I backed away. Paul Bunyan called and wanted his truck back, I thought, as he opened his door and clumsily dismounted. He was carrying a cup of coffee and a brown bag. He had a bandage over his nose and trust me, he wasn't smiling.

"Hey, Mr. Harbinger," I said, trying to ease the obvious tension.

He hurried past me and up to the front door. "Hold this, Bogart, and don't drop it." He handed me his coffee and his sack breakfast. Yeah, like I was going to just drop it? "You can't have your job back," he added as he opened the door and entered. I followed him into the building, still carrying his breakfast. The air-conditioner in the building must have been running all night because it felt nice and cool inside. It smelled musty and closeted, like the inside of a motel room. The sweat on my face and on the small of my back felt suddenly cold. But in a good way. It was nice compared to the heavy heat and humidity outside.

Harbinger didn't really walk. He lumbered, kinda like it was hard to lift up each foot and even harder to put each foot down. As I followed him down the hall to his office, I noticed just how genuinely poor his posture was. He slouched his shoulders and his feet leaned in, like he was trying to touch the insides of his shoes to the ground. He probably needed some foot wedges or something.

"Why're you here?"

"To pay for the septic tank."

He tossed his keys onto the desk as he went into his office and snatched his breakfast from my hands. He sat down, pulling his food out of the bag. It smelled good, like home cooking. The brown bag crunched each time he reached in and pulled something out—eggs in a plastic container, hash browns, a cup of orange juice, a couple of pieces of bread wrapped in foil, more hash browns, jelly, butter, syrup (good grief, I thought, how much can one man eat), and a couple of pancakes. I stood there in the doorway watching him spread out everything in front of him, like he had been waiting for that breakfast his whole fat, disfigured, sunburned life or something.

I stepped forward and put the cash on this desk. "Five hundred, like you said yesterday." He counted the money and then kept eating.

"As a matter of fact, Bogart," he said, "I didn't expect you to have the money so soon." Harbinger used the word "fact" as much as possible. Like that made him sound right or something. He'd say "in fact" or "as a matter of fact" or "the fact that I even have to ask you again," and "fact: you're in my way" or "the fact is…" or my favorite, "factually speaking."

"Factually speaking," Harbinger was saying now, "I've got some good news and some bad news. What do you want first?"

"How about the bad—"

"—all right, I'll start with the good. The fact of the matter is, the good news is that I'll take your money and that I'm not pressing charges for what you did to my nose."

"I didn't do that to your nose. The shovel did."

"Fact is, that's your side of the story."

"Then what's the bad news?"

"You've got three seconds to get off the property, Bogart, before I call the cops on your trailer-trash ass."

Fifteen

I ran away from Mulwray Headquarters. Getting arrested was the last thing I wanted. Since I needed a place to go so that Aunt Mel would think I was off working, I went to Jackson's house, which was a real dump 'cause they had like fifteen folks living there.

After Jackson got up and had his cereal, he gave me the rundown about the gambling ring. He told me not to look like I was trying to "make" anyone. "Make" them as in recognize them from a police picture or something. "I think some of them are criminals," Jackson said. "So don't ask them too many personal questions. Just keep to yourself, and don't act like a kid."

"I'm not some kid, Jackson. Don't forget who taught you everything you know about cards."

"A lot of good it's done me," he said.

"That's not my fault."

We were standing in the broom closet on the first floor, the only private room in his house. It was so dark in there that I couldn't even see Jackson's face. In every room we had entered, there'd been some member of Jackson's extended family playing dominos or reading scripture or watching television or yelling into the phone. So we'd resorted to the broom closet. After several minutes, I was starting to feel a little weird. I think it was the pungent odor of cleaning solvents and detergents.

He told me how there were always new faces at the game, but that the regular players were the ones I had to watch out for. "They're good," he said. "And they know how each other plays pretty well. You'll have an advantage at first, but eventually they'll figure your shit out. This is what some of them do for a *living*."

"Do you smell that?" I replied.

Jackson sniffed.

"Did you kick over some of that cleaner or something? Is that paint thinner?" I asked.

"It does smell pretty bad in here."

"Can we just get this conversation over with so that we can get out?" I buried my nose in the crux between my forearm and my excuse for a bicep. "I'm not worried. I know how to play and I know the codes."

"Fine, but if they ask you how old you are, tell them that you're, like, twenty or something."

"Actually, I was going to tell them I was twelve."

I hung out with Jackson for a couple of hours and then he had to go to work—that is, taxi folks around Ambricourt. Since I couldn't go with him, I went to hang out at the Walking Jay.

I got pretty drenched on the walk over to the Jay 'cause it was raining. I tried to hide in this giant ditch and wait it out. In one of those large, metal drainage tunnels. It smelled awfully musty in there. I had to stand up on the side and hunch over or split my legs above the steady stream of water that ran down the middle so as not to get my shoes soaked. I couldn't see too far back into the sewer on account of it being so dark. I yelled a couple of times. A few choice obscenities. I even sang part of *Amazing Grace*. It was the only song I could remember the words to.

The echo was amusing at first, but then it got old. And after a while, I got kinda spooked because I got to thinking that there might be a gator in there or something worse. Those are the types of stories you read about in the paper every so often. Kid attacked by alligator while hiding from the rain. I could imagine the slithering beast emerging from the darkness with its beady, blinking eyes and swinging tail, grabbing hold of my little legs and dragging me into the murky water of the ditch. It was going to be an epic struggle between the gator and me, but I was going to lose. At least probably an arm or a leg. So I got the hell out of there and continued walking to the Jay in the rain. Being a little wet was better than being an amputee.

It was almost five o'clock when I finally showed up at the Walking Jay. I read the whole newspaper and then I played a couple of games of solitaire by myself. I started doubting my decision not to tell Aunt Mel about getting fired. But before I felt guilty enough to decide to come clean, Mathers slid into the booth across from me with an urgent announcement.

"I was reading the paper the other day, Jim, and do you know what I learned?" he blurted out. "I learned they found a new planet. Yep, a new one!" he announced to the whole place. One or two people looked over.

I shrugged and took a sip of coffee—I needed to be wide awake, especially if the card game went into the early hours of morning. I thought that falling asleep would be a lousy way to make a first impression.

"Can you believe that?" he went on. "It was up there the whole time and we didn't even know it."

"What's that got to do with me, Mathers?"

"It all matters."

"All of what matters?"

"Everything and everyone," he whispered.

In the last few weeks, Mathers had started forgetting a lot of stuff and not making at least some sense. I'm not talking about obscure scientific discoveries—I'm talking about not-knowing-where-the-hell-he-is forgetting and not making sense. "What do you mean?"

"Well," he started, "the article said that the person who discovered the planet was not even a scientist, but one of the interns. What if that intern hadn't shown up for work that day, eh?"

"Yeah, that's true," I said as I stood up. "That planet might not have been discovered and then what would we have to talk about? There's my ride."

"Yep," he said.

I grabbed up my cards and wrapped them in the rubber band. Mathers looked at them. "Like those cards," he said. "When you play, every card matters. The lowest card can be just as important as the highest card."

I thought Mathers was getting a little too philosophical for the Walking Jay. "Well, I'll try and remember that," I said as I hurried toward the front door.

Sixteen

Jackson was slouched down behind the wheel. Every window in the car was rolled down.

"What took you so long?" I asked.

"Would you rather walk?"

"Don't forget I'm doing you the favor."

Without looking, he pulled out a pack of cigarettes and lit one. He turned over the ignition, but the car didn't start. "Come on, come on," he whispered several times, trying to keep the cigarette from falling from his lips into his lap.

The engine finally chortled, cranked, turned, and started, and Jackson maneuvered the great behemoth out onto the road.

We drove for a while.

Jackson smoked two cigarettes.

I looked out the window at the blurry landscape. I wasn't really looking at anything. I mean, I knew we were passing marshes and swampland then a few shopping centers, but I just wasn't thinking about what I was seeing. It was all just passing before my eyes. I did that sometimes. I started thinking about what Mathers had said, how the smallest card could make the biggest difference. It seemed pretty true—I'd definitely been beaten when a low card washed up in the river.

"There's a couple more things you need to know before we get there," Jackson began.

"Are you serious?"

"First, if the cops show up, you're on your own and I'm out the window."

"Thanks."

"And these guys aren't your little cotillion prep school friends."

"Do I look scared?" I was a little scared, but I wasn't about to let on. Bluffing was not limited to playing cards. "And I never did cotillion," I said. I was getting pretty tired of Jackson talking down to me about the card game, especially when he'd lost all his money already. "I'm not some chump, y'know. I know how to handle myself at a table."

He glanced at me and took a long drag from his cigarette, then flicked it out the window. "Let's hope so, for both our sakes," he said.

Sycamore Street was one of those nice neighborhoods that had really gone to the toilet. It was one of the oldest areas in Ambricourt and one of the lowest—meaning that it was ten or fifteen feet below sea level. Every time a storm passed through, the whole area would flood. People got tired of repairing their house and over time moved away, leaving an entire neighborhood of huge, abandoned homes. It was a ghost town of old houses obscured by thick and heavy-growing bushes and trees. From the street view you really couldn't make out most of them. Only a chimney or roof or something like that. I know, chimneys in Florida? It's true—old people need heat for blood circulation and all.

We slowly drove down Barrier Avenue, the parallel street, and made two left turns to get onto Sycamore Street.

Jackson stopped the car and lit another cigarette. He peered out my passenger-side window. "Let's do this." Steering over a couple of palm branches, he turned into the driveway. There were some seriously stately stanchions flanking the entrance.

I took another one of Jackson's cigarettes and lit it.

"Where is everybody?"

"They're here."

And they were. As we slowly drove up the driveway, I saw several cars. Some nice, some real junkers.

It was then that I clearly saw the house for the first time

It was a partially destroyed, Mediterranean-style house with three floors. A large deck wrapped around the first level on the right side. The paint on the house was peeling. There were plenty of broken windows. There was a downed palm tree sticking out of the front window with its roots sticking up, covered in dirt.

I could smell citrus.

The detached garage had completely collapsed in on itself.

The house seemed to be surrounded in darkness. I didn't know if that was because the sun had gone down or because of all the overgrown trees, but the place looked pretty eerie.

There was a large grove of cypress trees on the side of the house, with plenty of Spanish moss to go around.

"Who's hosting this game, the prince of darkness?" I asked.

"I told you, I didn't pick the place. I mean, what did you expect them to do, run a racket out of the mayor's office?"

"But isn't there some place, I dunno, not so close to the gates of hell where we could play?"

Jackson laughed. "I was a little spooked at first too, but you get used to it."

About then, I thought that gambling on Sycamore Street was about the dumbest thing in the world. I mean, the parking lot of the Walking Jay worked just fine for me.

"Listen, if you're scared already, maybe it's not such a good idea…" Jackson trailed off.

"Please," I said as I got out of the station wagon.

Jackson got out and headed around back. "This way."

I flicked my cigarette away and followed after him.

There was a pool back there. It was full of water all right, but it was covered in dead leaves and branches and random shit from the neighborhood.

Jackson picked up a stick and stirred the murky pool water. The leaves swirled around. "I've been wanting to do that," he announced, satisfied.

"That's great," I said. "Now can we get this over with?"

He opened one of the two French doors and I followed him inside.

Seventeen

We walked through the biggest kitchen I'd ever seen. I followed Jackson down a hall and through the foyer. Surprisingly, there was still furniture in the house. I saw a table that looked like it was about to fall over. We entered a large dining room and then I noticed a dim light coming from up a set of stairs. I could hear footsteps shuffling around above us.

"Up here."

We walked up three flights of rickety old stairs and then down the hall. The light grew stronger, illuminating walls where I noticed some framed photographs. I tried to stop and look at them, but Jackson seemed to be in a hurry.

As we turned another corner, I saw light coming from under a large door at the end of the hall. And I heard voices.

Jackson knocked.

The door opened just a crack and Jackson said, "It's me." Then the door opened all the way.

A tall man with tanned skin and long brown hair and charcoal eyes stood there. His shoulders were broad, but hunched. He was wearing a seaman's cap and he was unshaven. He was definitely scary-as-hell looking. I felt a little tremor of fear pass through my body as we walked past him and into what was the master bedroom. He smelled like dirt.

The room was enormous. There was a large, round table in the center where normally a bed might have been, and a small table in the corner that was fully stocked with several bottles of vodka and gin and wine. There were three other card tables around the room in different places. There was also dark-looking mold growing up on the walls and in the corners. I tried the best I could to put that out of my mind.

There were candles conspicuously placed throughout the room, casting shadows and light everywhere. Obviously the electricity in the house didn't work. There was a gas lamp hanging above the center table that somebody had jimmy-rigged up there. I wondered what Harbinger might say about the place. Probably point out any rounded corners and vaulted ceilings and countertops and such.

There were nine men sitting at the table, smoking cigarettes and drinking. No women. All men. In total, I counted eighteen folks in the room. Most didn't look like they were winning.

Jackson took me to the large table in the center. "Everybody," he announced, "this is Jim." Boy, I thought, that was subtle.

The guys at the table all turned around, almost in unison. I couldn't have planned it more awkwardly, let me tell you.

Anyway, I waved. I heard a few grunts and nods of greeting.

"I'm Robert," the tall man with the seaman's cap said. His voice was coarse "How old are you, boy?" he continued.

"Twenty-two," I said.

"Yeah, right," he said dismissively. "You want something to drink?"

"Sure." What I really wanted was a glass of water and four aspirin. Maybe a wooden cross, to tell you the truth, and some holy water.

Jackson went over to one of the tables and made small talk with one of the younger-looking guys. I followed Robert over to the small table in the corner. I thought it was strange that he was wearing flip-flops.

"What'll it be?" he asked.

"Uh … beer."

Robert reached down and retrieved a bottle of beer from one of those little ice chests that have the button on the side that you have to press to open the top. He took the bottle and placed the cap against the table edge and slammed his palm down against it. The cap flew off and pinged against one of the walls. He handed me the bottle.

"Thanks."

"Don't mention it." Although Robert's voice was the gruffest thing I'd ever heard, there was something familiar about it, like I'd heard it before.

We were standing there, facing the large table with the nine players. Jackson was smoking a cigarette and going on and on about something, talking like he was in a motion contest or something, the way he was bobbing his head and moving his arms and all.

"Jackson told me that you like to play Hold'em."

Well, so much for the element of surprise, I thought. "Sorta, y'know, just for fun."

"That's what losers say."

I didn't like Robert's tone of voice. I didn't appreciate this criminal's condescension one bit. In fact, I thought he had a lot of nerve, considering he was shacking up in some old, run-down house running some lame, small-time operation for spending cash.

"I wouldn't know," I shot back. Gambling was all about posturing.

Robert laughed a crooked, pinched laugh. From the side of his mouth, he said, "So long as you brought enough money to see about it. Good luck, boy." He reached out his hand. I shook it sternly. And then he pulled back his shirt, and I saw a gun tucked into his baggy cargo shorts. "But don't go getting too lucky," he threatened.

I hadn't expected him to have a gun, especially since he was wearing flip-flops. Obviously my expression indicated as much.

Robert laughed. "I'm only half kidding," he said as he let his shirt cover the gun back up. "Chips?" he asked, abruptly changing the subject.

"Yeah."

"How much?"

"A grand." He looked at me, his eyes full of skepticism. I pulled out a wad of cash and handed it to him.

"You mind if I count it?"

"Go ahead."

Eighteen

When Robert finished counting the money, he pulled out a rack containing the chips. He counted out a thousand dollars worth and handed the chips to me. "The rack goes on the floor next to your chair," he said.

"Okay." But I already knew that.

I sat down at the table next to Jackson.

There were several mismatching, worn and frayed armchairs around the table. There were a couple of kitchen chairs and several crates. I was sitting on a leather ottoman. It was low and so I felt a little emasculated reaching up to the table.

Jackson offered me a cigarette and I took it.

That's when I noticed that nobody was talking. The conversation had completely died.

The silence was uncomfortable.

"The ante is ten and the big blind and small blind," Robert said, "are ten and five, respectively. After one hour they double and every half hour after that."

"What's the purpose of a blind, anyway?" Jackson wondered aloud.

A few folks at the table scoffed, in disbelief or out of irritation. I couldn't tell which.

Robert tilted his hat, incredulous. "Jim, why don't you tell him," he said.

I felt all eyes on me. "Uh, well, Jackson, they're meant to get the action going right away. So that you don't look at your cards and just muck every time. It keeps everyone honest."

"Good enough," Robert said, lighting a cigarette and righting his cap.

"Oh," Jackson said, and winked at me. And then I realized that he was just playing dumb so that I could look good. What he didn't realize was that I wanted them to think I was beginner. That way I could surprise them. Jackson should've known that. It was no wonder he'd lost all his money.

Robert wasn't playing. He was just pacing around the room, keeping everything in order. *Flip-flop, flip-flop.* He looked like he was searching for a reason to kick someone's ass or shoot someone with that gun in his shorts.

There was a guy directly across from me wearing dark sunglasses. I thought he looked awfully ridiculous, but I sure wasn't going to say anything to him about it. Cliff sat a few chairs over. He had a lazy eye. I'd be looking around or something and I'd see his eye glaring right at me. I knew it wasn't working properly and that Cliff wasn't meaning to look at me with his lazy eye, but it was still kinda strange. Cliff ended up being a pretty nice guy, though. Smiled and talked a lot despite the thing with his eye.

That first round didn't last too long. Seven folded out of the pocket or after the flop. Three of us played.

The flop was a 2♦, a 3♠, and a 6♠. I was holding an A♠ and a 4♠. I was sitting on a flush draw.

A friendly-looking, middle-aged man with narrow shoulders wearing a Banana Jack hat and Hawaiian shirt called. I called. Cliff raised. Banana Jack called and I called again. Banana Jack took forever to figure out what he was going to do. Finally, he called and we were set for the turn, a.k.a. "Fourth Street."

Cliff tossed out the turn. It was a 6♣. That wasn't too good for me. Somebody was sitting on a three of a kind and I still didn't have shit.

I called. Cliff raised twenty dollars. Banana Jack re-raised one hundred dollars.

I folded.

Cliff stared at Banana Jack for a full minute with his one good eye. "You're lucky I don't have two good eyes," he said as mucked his cards.

So Banana Jack bought the pot and smiled as he collected the chips from the middle of the table. "Maybe you should've thought about that before you sat down at the poker table. But that explains why you keep losing."

Robert chuckled.

Banana Jack chortled.

And Cliff laughed, too. "Good one," he said to Banana Jack. "Nice hat, by the way."

Nineteen

Jackson and I did really well at the table that first night. It helped a lot that I was the new player to the game, because nobody knew my ticks. My beats. My giveaways. They didn't know when I was bluffing or when I was semi-bluffing or not bluffing at all. That definitely played into my hand, because I bought the pot several times by pretending on certain deals to have a better hand than I really did. That way, I was able to scare other players into folding quickly when I didn't have but two lousy cards. (I couldn't do that every time, because they would have figured it out eventually and called my bluff.)

The five hours that Jackson and I spent at the house

on Sycamore Street went by pretty quickly. Most everyone was pretty good, especially Banana Jack and Cliff with the lazy eye.

When we finally got up to leave, I had almost twice as many chips as I did when I sat down.

Jackson drove me home that night excited as all get-out that I'd won his money back. He even swore that he wasn't going to gamble ever again.

"Really?" I asked.

"Well, not for money anyway," he replied.

We turned onto Route 5 and Jackson sped toward the Straits. It was a dark road, and even darker at night.

"What about me?" I asked.

"What about you?" he said, lighting a cigarette.

"Well, I was thinking that I've got to keep going, because you know I really need the money after what happened at work and all," I said.

He thought about it for a second and asked me if I'd tried to get another job.

"What good would that do?"

He didn't answer, and I knew it was because there wasn't a job in all of Ambricourt that was going to pay me more in three days than I could earn gambling on Sycamore Street.

"But what do you need me for?" he asked, like he didn't know already.

"I need you to keep taking me, tomorrow night and the next." I looked out the window.

"Not that I should be asking this necessarily," he said. "But are you sure that's such a great idea? I mean, didn't *you* say that the first rule of gambling is not to bet what you can't lose?"

"That's different. I don't have a choice."

"You could just tell Aunt Mel the truth and see what she says."

"No, I couldn't."

"It's not like it was your fault you got fired."

"I dug the hole. And it's not like it's just Aunt Mel. I've got to do this for myself."

"What if you lose?" he asked. "What then? You'll have nothing."

"I've got to try."

"You sure?"

"Goddamnit, will you take me or not?" I shouted. "You owe me."

"Geez, relax. Of course, I'll take you. Somebody get this guy a drink," he said to himself. "But I can't take you on Saturday night. Only tomorrow and Sunday. Saturday is my brother's birthday and we're supposed to be having this lame family thing."

"Deal," I said. After all, two nights were better than none.

We rode along in silence for a while. Well, I was silent, but Jackson was doing this annoying clicking sound with his tongue.

Jackson dropped me off at the Straits. He said what time he'd pick me up tomorrow, and left.

I walked back to my trailer. There was a strange moony glow over all the trailers. I didn't hear a noise. Nothing. Just my footsteps. My shuffling along the gravel.

When I got home, Aunt Mel was up, still staring out the front window at the trailer across the way. I told her good night, but she didn't move a muscle. I didn't know if she was even awake. I wondered if it was possible for her to be doing that in her sleep. She was standing there, teetering back forth like one of the huge blow-up advertisements that you see on top of buildings sometimes, announcing a grand opening or something.

It was almost two in the morning when I pulled the covers up over my head and fell asleep. I dreamt about playing cards that night, about running the table against Banana Jack and Cliff and that guy in the sunglasses.

It was a good dream, but that is all it was.

FRIDAY EVENING, AUGUST 29

Using advanced weather models, the National Hurricane Center predicts an increase in the storm's wind speed, rainfall, and overall intensity and issues tropical storm watches and warnings to all areas in the storm's path.

Twenty

Most of Friday was spent walking to and from the mall in Calumet City to buy a new shirt. I wasn't much of a shopper, but also didn't want to show up at the Wilmots' party wearing the same shirt I was wearing when I was still going to school at the Academy.

At the mall, I went into the first store I found and bought the cheapest shirt I could find. It was a little big. The short sleeves hung down to my elbows, which I hated. But it was on sale.

I ate lunch in the food court and watched folks for an hour after I finished my meal—partly 'cause I couldn't move, my stomach was so full, and partly 'cause folks were so fun to look at.

I put on my new shirt in the public bathroom and walked straight to Kathy's house.

Mr. Montgomery answered the door, slowly opening it as he backed up, staying hidden behind it. He had a fringe of curly brown hair around his mostly bald head and had one of those annoying faces that always had the same expression. His bushy eyebrows were always raised and he was always half smiling, like somebody just told him a secret or something. Actually, it was a little unsettling. If I woke up in the middle of the night and Mr. Montgomery was standing above my bed, I'd probably shit my pants.

"Hello, Jim. Come in."

"Sure, thanks."

Mr. Montgomery took me into the living room.

Kathy's house smelled like potpourri. Like it was manufactured in the basement. It was that potent.

There was a giant, shiny black piano in their living room. I sat down on the sofa and Mr. Montgomery stood next to the piano, all obvious like he wanted me to ask him to play something. He looked at the piano and then looked at me. I didn't say a thing. Then he cleaned some spot of dust off the piano and finally he sat down on the bench.

"I was just playing a little something before you arrived."

He played a couple of bars.

"You know what that was?" he asked me.

"No."

"Thelonious Monk."

"Did he play at the monastery or something, for all the others?"

"No, he wasn't a religious man, not in the traditional sense."

"Oh."

"One more for you."

Awesome, I thought. Mr. Montgomery played something else, which lasted an awkwardly long time. I just sat there with my hands in my lap while he kept playing on and on. Once or twice I thought the song was over and then it would pick back up. I wondered why parents were so strange. Then I thought about the sofa and I wondered if Mrs. Montgomery had picked it out. It had a girly pattern. And then I snatched up a book on the coffee table and looked at it. It was called *Architecture and the American House*. I opened it up and flipped through while Mr. Montgomery played on, seemingly for himself at that point. Eventually I closed the book and put it down.

"Okay, go," he said as he stopped playing and half turned around.

"Huh?"

"What composer?" Mr. Montgomery asked, smiling disconcertingly. I blurted the first person that came to my mind because I wanted him to turn the hell back around and point that funny face in the other direction.

"Chopin."

"Good. You remembered." I didn't, but what was the point of letting on.

Every time I went over to Kathy's and Mr. Montgomery was home, he did this to me, tested me on my ability to name the composer or musician. I don't know why; maybe it was a quiz to see if I was worthy to be hanging out with Kathy.

"Yep," I said. Where is Kathy already? I thought.

I slammed the car door shut while Kathy said good-bye to her dad. Then Kathy joined me in her car.

"Nice of you to show up. I don't know how much more I could have taken of your dad's playing," I said.

"Sorry, I didn't have anything to wear."

I looked at what she was wearing and wondered what she was talking about.

"I feel frumpy," she said as she cranked the engine and gunned it in reverse back down the driveway. The bumper scraped against the pavement and it was real loud. The scraping noise scared one of the neighbor kids who was playing street hockey.

Here's something about Kathy: she drove like a bat outta hell—it was like a war and every other car was an enemy. There was lots of screeching and slamming of the breaks and gunning the gas involved. She'd gone to the *I'm-gonna-speed-past-the-tractor-trailer-against-oncoming-*

traffic-and-yank-the-automobile-back-into-the-right-lane-at-the-very-last-instant school of driving.

My body lurched forward as she slammed on the brakes at the sudden appearance of the stop sign at the end of her street. I probably would've hit my face against the dashboard if it wasn't for my seat belt, which pressed into my chest and caused the blood to rush to my head.

She accelerated through the intersection and I gripped that handle on the roof of the car. It was a death grip, too.

"You ... look ..." My body was sorta cranking all over the place, so it was hard to spit it out. " ... Nice."

"You think so?"

"Yeah. I like ... that ... skirt." It was short, and that was cool.

The sun glared brightly through the windshield. I put down the visor and took a deep, air-conditioned breath. I loved the smell of the Freon.

"Do you want to put some music on?" she asked.

"If you want to."

"There's a CD case somewhere."

I found the CD case from under my seat and flipped through it, not really thinking about what music to put on the stereo because I was seriously considering telling her about getting set up by Hollis and fired by Harbinger. Though I decided against doing it there in the car, I made up my mind to tell her eventually—after I won the money Aunt Mel and I needed. It would be easier to accompany bad news (for example, "Hey Kathy, I've not been completely honest") with good news ("Hey Kathy, I'm a complete badass and I won all the money back"). More than anything, I just didn't want her to think I was some trailer-trash loser like Hollis said I was.

I put some random CD that I didn't even look at into the player. It turned out to be a recital CD of one of her father's students. I just couldn't get away from the guy.

"That's an interesting choice," Kathy said.

"Yeah," I said weakly. "We can listen to something else if you want."

"It's fine," she said, glancing my direction. "That's a cool shirt, is it new?"

"No," I replied, trying to sound cool. "I just haven't worn it in a while."

"It's nice," she said. "I especially like the price tag hanging out the collar."

I ripped out the tag, doing my best to conceal the clearance sticker.

She smiled and flirtatiously smacked my knee. "You're acting weird."

"Really? Maybe it's the music."

"Hey, that's one of my dad's students," she replied with a laugh. "Are you nervous about tonight or something?"

"Should I be?"

"No."

"I'm not nervous," I said, but it was obvious by the expression on her face that she wasn't buying it.

Twenty-one

Every summer, Mr. and Mrs. Wilmot went on a vacation. The weekend they were gone, one of their kids would throw a party. Their house was situated on prime real estate, between a golf course and the beach. Obviously, the Wilmots were pretty loaded.

Russ Wilmot was the youngest of five kids, and he'd been in my English class last year. His brother, Ben, graduated from the Academy last spring and he'd thrown one hell of a party during the summer, I heard, probably the best there ever was (each year they seemed to get bigger and better). The rest of the Wilmot kids had been in high school when I was just in grade school, so I never really knew them. Russ used to say the meanest things about his brothers and sisters, but then as soon as one of them showed up or something, you'd think Russ had forgotten everything he'd said because he'd grovel and act like he worshipped them, laughing at their stupid jokes which most of the time came at his expense.

Russ and I got on pretty well, but he was desperate to be popular and well liked and all of that crap. I didn't hold it against him, though. I just felt bad for Russ.

We used to play cards at recess. I even taught him a couple of tricks, mostly silly little sleight-of-hand stuff, but he seemed to like them. He'd lost a bunch of money to me in the gambling ring in ninth grade. I gave it back to him, though, because I felt so bad about it. I really wasn't playing for money. I just liked playing.

When Kathy and I got to the party, there were cars lined up and down the street. We had to park what seemed like a mile away. Each time Kathy passed a car owned by someone she knew, she said so. I didn't recognize very many cars, like two maybe.

We walked up to the front yard and, of course, Hollis' car was parked there, angled in the driveway so nobody could pull in next to him. I hated that about Hollis—the privileges he assumed were owed to him because he was rich. He was a lot richer than the Wilmots, but there's no way in hell his parents would let him throw a party.

The Wilmots' house was perfect for a party because it was far away from any other house so it didn't matter how loud everyone was.Nobody would care except the little crabs and such on the beach or the little lizards hiding under the brush on the golf course.

Kathy and I made our way up the front steps and to the front door.

"Wait," I said just before she opened the door.

She brushed the hair away from her shoulder. "What?"

There's not much that's worse than being the last one to join a crowded room. Like being late for class and you have to walk in there and everyone is sitting, just looking at you. I hadn't even seen most of my ex-classmates from Ambricourt Academy for going on a year, since after Hurricane Leland I'd finished the year at South Ambricourt High. It's not like the record was going to scratch and everyone and their sister was going to turn around when Kathy and I walked in, but I was still nervous about it. Standing there on the front porch with my hands shoved into my pockets, I was suddenly aware of how much I didn't want to be asked stupid questions about my mom or my sister or the Straits. "Maybe I'll just go wait in the car until you're ready to leave," I said.

She laughed and told me to shut up. "Nobody is going to even notice us come in."

"Just don't leave me, okay? I don't want to go in there and have you see someone you know and just ditch me, all right? I mean, I don't want to be that guy who has nobody to talk to and just stares off at the ocean pretending to be thinking about something important, okay."

"I never knew you were so uptight," she said.

"I'm not uptight."

She was wrong about that "nobody is going to notice us" stuff. When she opened the door, there were like fifty kids in the living room watching something on television—which happened to be somewhere near the front door, so they were all kinda facing us when we entered.

As Kathy greeted several girls and led me into the kitchen, I started mentally formulating some sort of game plan—who I was going to talk to and in what order, and what I was going to say to start the conversation and how I was going to get out of the conversation.

"Jim," I heard someone say as we entered the kitchen. "It's been a long time. I didn't know you'd be here."

I turned around and it was Mickey Douglas. He'd been the kid at recess who got called on last in that Red Rover game. That Red Rover game was always a good gauge for how popular everyone was. The first person called was always the coolest and most popular, and the last person called, in this case Mickey Douglas, was always the least popular. He always had a crew cut, which is what you might expect with a name like Mickey.

"Mickey," I said.

"How's it going?" he asked. He was holding a cup of beer in one hand and he raised the other as if he wanted to give me a high five.

"What is that up there for?" I asked, motioning toward his hand. That was one of the reasons why Mickey Douglas was unpopular; he never missed an inopportune time to give someone a high five. I didn't know how he got invited to the Wilmots' party.

"I was just kidding," he said and put his hand against the doorframe, as if that was what he was going to do in the first place. "How's the Straits? That must be rough, with your mom and sister dead and all. Kids still talk about your mom from time to time."

Another reason why Mickey wasn't all that popular was 'cause he had less tact than a tidal wave. I grimaced at Kathy and responded to Mickey without looking away from her. "Terrific," I said.

She smiled and said, "We'll see you later, Mickey. We're gonna get something to drink."

"Through there," he said as he pointed across the kitchen. As we walked away, I saw him salute us good-bye, real tough-like.

Kathy and I walked out onto the back deck and someone handed us a couple of beers. "That went rather well, don't you think?" I asked.

"Cheers," she said, ignoring my sarcasm.

The house lights illuminated the beach just enough for us to see the waves breaking against the shore. There was a humid breeze blowing.

"This is such a nice house," Kathy said. And she was right about that. Like most beach houses, this one was on stilts so that it could withstand storm surges, if and when they came. There were about four or five different sun decks and verandas extending out on each floor, all the way up to the top floor.

"This party seems pretty tame so far. Last year was fun. Remember last year, when all those people went skinny dipping?" she asked.

"I didn't go."

"I left early 'cause it was pretty stupid," she said, trying to make me feel better about not having gone.

The beer was mostly bitter foam. The only reason I kept drinking was because the cup was in my hand and I didn't feel like going to find a trash can.

"I wonder where Nancy is?" she asked, mostly to herself. "Probably with Hollis somewhere."

"Does she like him or something?"

"Oh, you know how she is."

Everyone sure as hell did know how she was, but for the sake of not coming across like a total jerk, I decided against stating the obvious. In life as in poker, you don't show what you don't have to.

"I wonder if Charlie's here," she said.

Charlie Bryant was another one of my friends from the Academy. I hadn't heard from him since last year, not since Hurricane Leland.

"Do you wanna go find him?" she asked.

"We're not friends."

"Oh, come on."

"I'm serious," I said.

I really didn't care all that much about him anymore. I sure as hell didn't need to resuscitate a dead relationship.

"Well, I'm going to go to the bathroom. Where are you going to be?" she asked matter-of-factly.

"What? Don't leave me already."

"Seriously, Jim," she said, and turned around and went inside, leaving me alone on the deck.

Twenty-two

So much for not being left alone. I almost wished Mickey would come up and ask me more stupid questions that I didn't want to answer.

I finished my beer and got another one. After I finished that one, I got one more.

There were a couple of kids I didn't recognize out on the deck smoking cigarettes. I thought about asking for one, but I didn't want to be *that* guy.

I stood there for a couple of minutes looking out at the ocean, trying to appear mentally occupied so that nobody thought I was just looking out at the ocean because I had nobody to talk to. I looked down at the sand and wondered what would happen if I somehow fell off the deck—if I'd get hurt or not. I wondered if the supports holding up the deck were strong enough to withstand the weight of everyone on it.

And then I started to feel goddamn dizzy. So I decided to go inside and take a look around and find Kathy. After exploring the lower levels, I went upstairs, grabbing another beer on my way. The party seemed to be getting bigger because I could barely squeeze through the hallway. I accidentally knocked off one of the family pictures and broke the frame. I hung it back up, broken frame and all.

On the top floor, I reached what appeared to be the master bedroom. It was enormous. I slowly walked through it and, for some reason, felt the density of the bed. I looked at a couple of pictures on the dresser. Russ wasn't photogenic at all. And for that matter, none of the Wilmots were. I went out on the deck—slid open the glass door and just stepped out. I probably wouldn't have done it in the first place if I wasn't a little tipsy.

It was pretty high up there. I didn't go near the railing because I didn't have to. I could hear kids screwing around down below. Even from where I was standing, away from the edge, I could see Kathy down on the beach. She was walking away from a group of kids that included Hollis, Nancy, and Vera and Jesse Danner. She was headed back toward the house and I wondered what she had been talking to them about. I was sure she told them she'd come with me. And I was sure Hollis was pissed. I smiled at the very thought.

I finished off my beer and for the hell of it, shot it like a basketball over the edge of the deck.

"Litterbug," I heard a voice say, behind me. I turned around. It was Russ. He had a half empty bottle of whiskey next to him. He was reclining drunkenly in an Adirondack chair.

"Russ. I didn't see you there."

"I know." He lit a cigarette and coughed.

"When did you start smoking?"

"Right now, actually."

"What's the occasion?"

He thought about it. His eyes were kinda glazed over. He started to answer and then stopped. Then he said, "I haven't seen you in a long time, Jim, like a year at least."

"Likewise."

"Have a seat," he said with all the enthusiasm of someone about to pass out. "You want some?"

"Sure, why not." I loathed whiskey. "Pretty good party, eh?"

"It's okay."

"There are tons of kids here."

"You know what I remember?" he said. "I remember that time you told my brother Ben to screw off."

"Then you said the same thing to me," I pointed out. I took a swig of whiskey and thought I was going to die.

He laughed, coughing at the same time. "Sorry about that."

"It's okay. I would've done the same thing if someone had said that to my sister. I mean, I just thought Ben was being an asshole 'cause you did that trick pretty well."

I sat down on the other Adirondack chair. And looked at drunk Russ. I felt bad for him. A minute or two passed before we spoke again.

"You still play cards?"

"Now and again."

"Remember when you got busted for the gambling ring? You were really kicking ass."

"Yeah, I remember." I couldn't believe he hadn't passed out yet. His head kept kinda teetering there on his shoulders and his eyes kept closing on him. He offered me another sip of whiskey, which I waved off.

"My brothers and sisters were supposed to come tonight, y'know," he continued. "They said they'd help with the planning, too."

I felt bad for Russ. Real stinking bad. He flicked his cigarette over the side of the deck. I heard someone say, "What the hell?" Russ must've heard it too because he smiled to himself, amused. It was the smile of an intoxicated stupor, the smile of a drunken heartbreak, the smile of a lonely boy growing into a broken man right before my eyes.

"I'm glad you came, Jim. You were always nice to me even though I wasn't always that cool to you."

"Don't worry about it. I had a good time teaching you

those card tricks, remember? And beating you at spades."
He laughed and then stopped, staring off into the fog of
god knows what. This conversation was getting a little
heavy for my liking, and I wanted to leave and go down-
stairs and find Kathy and get mad at her for leaving me.
I sure as shit didn't want to stay up on that deck and get
depressed with Russ.

As if he could read my mind or something, he asked if
I would go get him a beer. "Gladly," I said

"Jim?" he began. I had already gotten up and gone
inside. I was about to close the door. "D'you ever think
about what if it was you in that house and not your sister
and your mom?"

I leaned out, placed my hands on the door and the
wall, my back arching at the shoulder blades. I didn't know
what he was getting at but I said, "Sometimes," so he didn't
think I was being antagonistic. And then for some reason I
walked over and patted him on the shoulder like we were
best friends or something, like it had been years and years
since we'd seen each other and this was a chance encounter
in some alley in the middle of the night, as he was coming and I was going and we were moments from parting
company yet again. Something like that. Then he asked if
I believed in an afterlife.

I thought about it for a second and then I said, "Yeah,
and I can't wait for it. The world we live in is full of suffer-
ing and misery and pain. This house you got? It's beautiful

and big and all, and mine is ugly and small and . . . *mobile*, but they're just . . . different cells of the same prison."

"Is that in a book?" he asked with an eager, plaintive expression.

"The way I look at it," I said, "the faster we run over the burning coals, the faster we get through life, the better—the less pain we have to feel. It's always better to get it over with. And I hope our next life is nothing like this one." Maybe I was laying it all on a little thick, but up until that point I'd been so agreeable to Russ and it was like my disagreeable side had just boiled over.

I left Russ up there to ruminate over what I hadn't articulated all that well while I went to get him a drink. Honestly, I didn't have any intention of going back up there to take him that beer. It was just too depressing. I was liable to start crying or something.

Twenty-three

"Where were you?" I asked Kathy as I ran into her on the lower deck.

"I went to tell Nancy we were here," she responded.

"Thanks for ditching me. I just had the most depressing conversation."

"With who?" And then Kathy looked up. And then I noticed that everybody was looking up and pointing and making gasping noises. I figured I should look up too, so I did, and I saw Russ standing up there on the railing.

"Him, actually," I said.

Russ was awfully wobbly and I knew he was going to jump. I reckoned he took what I'd said literally and not on the theoretical level. Had I known he was in such a bad way, I would've held my tongue. He looked down at everyone and then he looked out at the ocean. And then he did it.

He misjudged his falling ability, 'cause he landed on the deck six feet below with a loud thump. He just disappeared out of sight behind the railing. From where I was standing, it looked kinda funny. A couple of guys ran up there to tend to him. Russ had just tried to kill himself and only two kids went to see if he was okay, I thought. I wondered how many kids would see if I was okay if I had just done that. Probably just Kathy and maybe Mickey. I didn't know what I'd do if I was dying and Mickey came to see if I was okay. I'd be pissed.

"Should we go see if he's okay?" Kathy asked.

"They've got it covered," I said flatly. I was starting to feel drunk about then.

"The line for the beer just cleared, you want another?" she asked. I couldn't tell if she wanted to get the beer herself or if she wanted me to do it for her. I didn't understand girls. They wanted you to open the door for them and then they wanted to tell you that they could have done it for themselves. That didn't make sense to me, but what the hell, right? So Kathy and I stood there for a second while I thought about all of this. And when I forgot what I was supposed to be thinking about, I just stepped up and gave that pump a couple of good cranks and filled up two cups of beer.

"Thanks," she said. "But I could have gotten it." Oh, yeah, that's what I was thinking about, I thought. "You wanna go for a walk?" I asked.

"Well, maybe we should—"

"Oh, come on," I said. "Let's just go look around."

"Okay," she said. "But not for long."

Kathy and I squeezed our way back through the hall toward the living room. I saw some random dude standing there with the broken picture frame. He must've knocked it off the wall like I did.

"You're so busted," I said as I brushed past. He looked up at me with one of those looks that a dog gives you when they're taking a dump, the *doing-this-in-the-front-yard-is-bad-enough-without-you-watching-me-do-it* look.

"Where's the bathroom?" I asked Kathy. "I need to wash my hands."

"Through there."

There was someone in the bathroom when I got there. So I waited and waited and finally Mickey came out. He had this lame smile on his face and when I went into the bathroom I figured out right away why he was smiling all right. The smell hit me like a speeding train hits a hay pile. That was some rank and rarified air in there. Smelled so bad I thought I was going let my stomach go. I didn't know what the hell Mickey ate, but it did some number on his bowels. Out of the fire and into the flames. I pulled my shirt up over my nose and washed my hands and got the hell outta there.

Hollis was standing right there when I opened the door. Mickey's wickedness wafted through the air, escaping around me, right to his nose.

"What the hell!" He buried his face in his shoulder.

I didn't answer. Because what could I say?

"Is that human? Did you really make that?" Hollis asked. "That's goddamn rank!" I knew Hollis was enjoying himself. I just knew it.

"Mickey did it, not me." I pointed in some arbitrary direction with my thumb.

"Yeah, right. Who invited you, anyway?" Hollis announced. He stepped closer to me and whispered, "I thought I told you no trailer honky-tonk trash allowed!"

"You did tell me. I just ignored you."

"And now you're going to regret it," he seethed, pushing me in the chest.

Before I could push him back, Kathy stepped between us. "Stop! Hollis, I invited him."

I'd never seen Kathy and Hollis in an argument. It was pretty cool.

Nancy grabbed Kathy by the elbow. "Calm down."

"Yeah, calm down, *Kat*," Hollis said.

She hated that nickname.

What happened next was unbelievable. Kathy took out the gum she was chewing on and slapped the back of Hollis' head and rubbed it in. Then she grabbed me by the arm and practically dragged me back into the living room and out the front door.

That was awesome, I thought. I hadn't seen gum used as a weapon since I was a little kid.

Twenty-four

Kathy and I walked over to the golf course, to the green of the seventeenth hole. I think it was a par three. I lay down on my back and bent my knees, putting my feet flat on the trim grass. She took her sandals off and crossed her legs.

She sighed. "Sometimes he can be such an elitist jerk, y'know."

"Wow, a real lover's quarrel," I mocked.

"We're not lovers!"

"You could've fooled me."

She jumped up and put her hands on hips. "You're kidding, right?"

"No."

"Me and Hollis?"

"Everyone knows it."

"We're just friends." She sat down grudgingly and stretched out her legs, leaning back on her elbows. "It's cool out here," she said. I wasn't listening, though. I was looking up at the stars wondering if my mom and Martha were looking down at me right then.

"How'd you do in school this year?" she asked.

"All right," I said. "It was easier than at the Academy."

I could smell Kathy's perfume, lilac or something. It was intoxicating and I was lost in it. Then I wondered if I had beer breath. I pretended like I was yawning and cupped my hand around my mouth so that I could smell my own breath. It didn't work.

"Are you tired?" she asked.

"Not really, you?"

"No," she said as she adjusted herself. "I've gotta get up early tomorrow."

"Why?"

"I'm counting endangered sparrows at Lake Hales Preserve."

"That sounds ... terrible, actually."

She laughed. "It's fun. I've been doing it for the last several weeks. I didn't tell you?"

"I would've remembered the image of you walking around the preserve counting birds."

"Do you want to go?"

"What does it require of me?" I asked.

"Not much. Just show up, basically. It's pretty easy. Do you want to? It'll be fun."

I smiled. "Are you asking me out on a date?"

"Ha, ha," she said, and kicked me harder than she realized because it kinda hurt like hell. "I'm serious," she said.

I still needed a place to be during the daytime so Aunt Mel would think I was working for Mulwray. "I'll think about it," I replied. But I didn't need to think about. I knew I wanted to. After all, I'd be spending the whole day with Kathy.

We were silent for a few minutes, both of us sorta looking off into the night sky.

Kathy spoke up. "Nights like this, I miss my mom."

Nights like this, I feel like really getting it on with you, I thought. "Me, too," I said.

"When I was a little girl, my mom and I used to sit on the porch at night and we'd imagine that we were a hundred years back in time looking up at the stars in the sky. The sky hasn't changed all that much. Back then they were probably looking at basically the same constellations as we are right now."

Staring up at the stars with Kathy, feeling insecure about my beer breath but intoxicated by the smell of lilac, I felt really sad and really safe and really comfortable.

"Do you ever wanna talk about *your* mom and sister?" she asked softly, slowly.

"Uh, no."

"If you ever want to," she said, "you can talk to me."

"Uh, I know."

"Talking about my mom makes me feel better about not having one."

A few minutes later, we repositioned, lying side by side.

"Did you know they've discovered a new planet?" I asked.

"What?"

"Mathers told me that."

"That old guy at the Jay who freaks everyone out?"

"That's him," I said.

"I like that you're nice to him," she said.

I didn't know how to respond. So I didn't. But I felt her edge a little closer to me. She did it casually, like she was just moving her elbow or something. But I felt her arm next to mine. And I know she felt it too. Neither of us moved for a long time after that. I'd never felt so close to anyone as I did lying there on the golf course with Kathy. My feelings for her seemed more intense, more real than ever. It was overwhelming, like going all in on a pair and then making four of a kind on the river. Even more overwhelming than that.

We didn't talk much on the way home, mostly just listened to music with the windows down. I wished I could've told her about what I was doing on Sycamore Street, but I knew she'd never understand. Not in a hundred star-filled years would she understand.

Kathy dropped me off at the entrance to the Straits and as she drove away, I stood there looking after her taillights, wondering if I had time to get a snack at my trailer before Jackson picked me up.

Twenty-five

I didn't like leaving Aunt Mel home by herself. Especially since the Straits wasn't exactly the safest place in the world. In the last month, there'd been a number of break-ins and thefts. Vandalism was pretty much the standard. Sometimes Ms. Rodriguez came over, but that didn't happen often. Ms. Rodriguez had two jobs because, like us, she was trying to save up enough money to find an apartment of her own by the deadline. And she had three kids, so she was in a real fix. She always looked like hell.

Rain began to fall as I walked back through the Straits. It wasn't coming down hard—just every now and then I felt a drop land on my head or my arm.

I entered the trailer slowly, quietly, wondering if Aunt Mel was asleep or—

"Hey, Jim," Aunt Mel said. She was over by the window, looking out.

"Hey."

"I just dropped off another batch."

"Aunt Mel, do you seriously think we can actually afford you spending time and money baking for the neighbors?"

Aunt Mel didn't miss a beat. "Oh, it doesn't cost that much."

"Are you sure? I mean, there's the gas, the ingredients, the time it takes you to do all that when you could be tying knots. That seems like a lot to me."

"I'm doing the best I can here," she said defensively.

I let it go and grabbed something from the fridge. Even though it didn't make one iota of practical sense, everybody needed something to accomplish—something that meant they mattered—and if seeing the neighbors was Aunt Mel's *something*, so be it.

Twenty-six

It was raining pretty hard when we got to Sycamore Street later that night. Jackson and I jumped out of the wagon express and ran up around the back of the house. I didn't even notice how many cars were parked in the driveway.

Into the house and up the stairs and down the hall as fast as we could.

Jackson knocked. Robert opened the door and let us in. And I about lost my lunch when I saw who was standing in the corner.

Hollis Mulwray.

He looked proudly at Jackson and me. His beautifully

spiked hair was completely shaved off. Because of what Kathy had done with the gum, no doubt.

Hollis came up to me as I was exchanging my money for chips.

"What're you doing here?" he asked, sounding as if he already knew the answer.

"That's funny. I was going to ask you the same question."

"You two know each other?" asked Robert, who was standing between us.

Hollis smirked. "We used to work together."

"Small world," Robert said.

I didn't say anything. Jackson piped in. "Nice haircut. Be all you can be, soldier."

Hollis grinned. "You better watch these two. Make sure they keep their hands above the table."

"I'm pretty good at reading people," Robert said as he looked suspiciously at Jackson and me and Hollis, and then walked away.

"I thought you would be at the party," I said.

"I left," he snapped.

"You mean, after Kathy stuck gum in your hair?"

"Ha ha," he grumbled sarcastically.

"How'd you even find out about this place?" Jackson asked him.

"Some of us ended up at the Walking Jay after the party. That crazy guy with missing teeth, what's his name?"

"Mathers?" I offered.

"Yeah, him."

"Son of a bitch," Jackson said. "He must've overheard us talking it."

"So what, then—you think you're gonna come here and beat me or something?" I taunted.

"And settle once and for all who is the best." People like Hollis would go to any length to prove they were better than people like me.

"Is there a problem?" Robert came up behind us.

"Not at all," I said confidently.

"Good," he replied, eyeing the three of us. "Then let's play."

I played pretty tight all evening because there was this new guy there named Cheepo. That was his name. I'd never seen anyone play cards the way he did. He was constantly talking about this or that, not afraid to say anything to anyone. He was this short, stubby guy with beady old eyes. He kept referring to himself in the third person, in this squeaky voice. "Cheepo's got two aces in the hole. Cheepo's going to win. Cheepo lost. Cheepo wants a drink." And then he'd just say his name just for the hell of it: "Cheepo. Cheepo."

It really knocked Hollis out of his game, I think. Hollis played cards like a rock; he was pretty tight with his chips, only playing when the cards were in his favor. He was also a steamer, someone who gets riled really easily, especially after losing a couple of big hands. And toward the end of the night, when Hollis lost to Cheepo, it was goddamn hilarious. Everyone at the table was laughing. Cheepo's hole cards were a 10♣ and a 10♠.

"Cheepo's got a pair of tens. Cheepo," he said to everyone. "What does Hollis have?"

Hollis had a bottom pair with two fives in the hole.

The flop was a 7♦, a 6♥, and a 4♦.

Thinking that Hollis may have flopped a straight, Cheepo put out a low feeler bet. Hollis called, revealing nothing to Cheepo about the strength of his cards.

The turn gave up a 10♥. So now Cheepo had three of a kind, but he still had to assume Hollis had a straight.

Then, for the first time all night, Hollis went all in, thinking that he could scare Cheepo into thinking he had a straight when, in fact, he only had a pair. Hollis needed a 3 or an 8 to wash up in the river to connect for the straight.

Well, Cheepo thought about the amount of money in the pot and considered the chances of Hollis bluffing and decided that the correct play, regardless of the outcome, was to call, and so he did. To win, Cheepo needed to pair the board with a 7, 6, or 4 in the river (which would give him a full house) or spike the tens—to get all four tens.

"Cheepo calls. Cheepo." And Cheepo pushed his chips in.

Hollis flipped over his low pair of fives and Cheepo flipped over his pair of tens.

Cheepo smiled.

So there they were, facing off with about $2,000 in the pot, and then the river came and it was a 6♥, which gave Cheepo a full house and the pot. Cheepo was all smiles and Hollis just stared at the table, his eyes wide and unflinching.

"Cheepo!" Cheepo offered as he raked in the chips.

"Shit!" Hollis stood up and kicked his chaired across the room.

Everyone turned around, startled.

Jackson and I looked at each other, both smiling from ear to ear.

The whole way home, Jackson and I laughed at Hollis and how he lost to Cheepo's full house. After Hollis left Sycamore in a huff, I didn't play very well—I barely grinded out breakin' even. I didn't lose any money, but I didn't win any, either.

Breaking even wasn't going to get us out of the Straits.

I needed to win and win big, and time was running out.

Saturday Morning, August 30

Satellites indicate a change in the tropical storm's direction from west to north, northeast.

Infrared and Doppler radars show a significant decrease in wind speed and precipitation. Experts predict the storm to die at sea and not reach the land.

Twenty-seven

I t's about time," she said.

I was standing on Kathy's front porch, half asleep and not feeling terribly up to counting sparrows at Lake Hales. I was just balancing there. I felt my legs a little weak under me. So if a strong gust of wind had come along, I would have toppled right over.

"I thought you were going to be here at eight," she continued.

"I thought I was too." I rubbed my eyes. "Sorry. I reckon that was a bit ambitious—"

"Come on," she said as she stepped past me.

It was about 8:30 AM. I'd slept through my alarm for

half an hour. Then I'd gotten up in a fury when I saw it was 7:45 AM. Walking over to her house in a total daze because I was so tired, I was almost hit by a car once or twice because I wasn't paying any attention.

We got in the car and Kathy peeled out of the driveway. At least she'd make up some lost time during the drive.

"This isn't going to look good on my first day," I pointed out.

"Really?" she quipped.

"No."

The piano-recital music was still in the stereo. It was too early in the morning for that so I turned it off.

We were driving on a four-lane highway, and they were paving one of the two lanes on our side. The lane that had been repaved was a couple inches higher than the other lane—which was all bumpy and rough. Kathy kept maneuvering around cars, so we'd go up one lane and then down onto the other with a *thump, thump* as the tires rolled up and down the uneven pavement. The freshly paved lane was smooth and quiet and peaceful. The older lane was loud and obnoxious and rough. But all of the up and down, up and down, thump, thump business was making me sick. I asked her if she could just pick a lane and stick with it, and she said that if I hadn't made us late, maybe she could have.

Kathy did a partially controlled careen off the highway and I rolled down my window. Her hair was blowing everywhere, but she didn't seem to mind. She didn't even try to pull it out of her face. She just didn't care. I thought she looked awfully hot like that.

We finally got to the Lake Hales Nature Preserve. We signed in and Kathy introduced me to this woman who had this matching khaki outfit on—shorts, shirt, and hat. She looked like she'd just returned from a safari. Her name was von Vanderkamp. Ellen von Vanderkamp. I asked if I could called her Ellen because von Vanderkamp was a mouthful. She said that I couldn't, smartass. Kathy later told me that if I'd been *on time*, we could have met Pablo Ellroy, a really sweet Cuban man with dark curly hair. I asked her if all the employees of Lake Hales had communist leanings. She didn't know, but told me to shut up about it. And then I asked her what kind of Cuban has a name like Ellroy? She told me the kind that could kick my ass. She said it kinda flirty, though.

It was after ten o'clock when we stepped outside with our odd-looking reflector vests and our oversized clipboards and our walking sticks and our whistles. We had water bottles, too. Since it was my first time, Vanderkamp had talked to me for a long time about what to do and what not to do. I even had to listen to this tape with different bird sounds so that I would know how to hear the sparrows. That didn't do a lick of good. Who knew birds could put you to sleep so fast? Vanderkamp also went on and on about how terrific the Florida Ornithological Society was. She said that one day I could become a member if I wanted to. I told her not to hold her breath, and that didn't go over very well.

Kathy and I left the administration area and walked down a gravel path. Kathy was explaining how field sparrows are often silent around their nests and how they're insectivorous during summer. I was wondering if she'd like me more since I was counting sparrows with her.

"Are you listening to me?" she asked, as we stepped from the path into the scrub.

"Yeah, but how do we know if we're counting sparrows that somebody else has already counted? After all, they do fly around."

"We won't know for sure," she said nonchalantly. "But the sparrows we're after don't go too far from their nests, which is why the preserve is divided into a grid system."

"Like the Straits?"

"Actually, yeah. Sorta," she said and pointed to the paper on her clipboard. "That's why there are so many questions on this form to answer after we spot one. So after all the information is compiled, an adequate estimation can be made as to how many sparrows are actually here."

"So what you're saying is, after we do all this, we're still not going to know for certain how many sparrows there are?"

She thought about it for a second and then smiled. "Basically."

Twenty-eight

Kathy and I talked all morning long, about things I hadn't thought about in a long time, deliberately or otherwise. There was something about Kathy that made me feel like it was okay to say out loud some of the things I had a hard time even thinking about. I even told her about the times my mom and Martha and me went to Valdosta, Georgia, to visit Aunt Mel. That was before Aunt Mel got divorced for the third time and moved to Ambricourt.

I loved packing up everything and going on a road trip, even as a kid. I'd fold myself into that space on the floor between the back of the front seat and the front of the back seat. I'd have my pillow and my books and my playing cards and it was a real kick-ass time, down there where nobody could see you.

The idea of vacationing in Valdosta was always better than the actual vacation. Mel and my mom would inevitably start bickering about what was going on in my mom's life. Not exactly the prelude to a great time, if you know what I mean.

Martha and I would always get bored out of our minds. We'd sit around on beanbags watching television or something, and then go fishing and never catch anything because the bread balls we used for bait never stayed on the hook. Our spit just wasn't sticky enough.

The two of us did almost everything together, especially during the summer. (At least, when she wasn't getting away from me, running off to go explore or talk to some stranger.) We'd go hiking around the woods or build forts or have water fights. Aunt Mel's neighbors had one of those yellow Slip 'N Slides. We played on that thing every day until some kid slipped and *slided* a little too far and dragged to a stop halfway down the sidewalk. He went crying bloody murder all the way home, bleeding from his elbows and knees. The year after that, Martha and I couldn't wait to go back to Aunt Mel's to play on that slide again. But the kids who owned it had moved away.

Kathy and I didn't see very many sparrows to begin with. At least, *I* didn't. I heard plenty of them, or I thought I did, but there's a world of difference between knowing the sparrows are somewhere out there and actually accounting for them.

I saw a couple of birds—the Northern Mockingbird, which is the Florida state bird, and a Treecreeper and what Kathy said was a Carolina Wren. The first sparrow I saw was dead. There were maggots or something festering around the insides. Flies buzzed about. It looked like it had been dead for a while. Rotting there all alone. I wondered how it had died—if it just died of natural causes. What is a "natural cause" for a sparrow to die? That's a question you don't hear often.

We stood there in silence for a few seconds and then I suggested we bury the thing. There was a nearby ditch so I just sorta pushed the sparrow into the ditch with a stick. Then I covered it with leaves and branches and stuff. Obviously, neither of us had a shovel and we weren't that enthusiastic about touching it with our bare hands.

"Does that one count?" I asked. "Can I mark it down on my sheet?"

"It was dead," she said.

"That's the first one I've seen, though."

"I don't think that one counts," she smiled competitively.

"I see how it is."

"Fine, mark it down."

"No, no," I said. "I won't count it if it's that important you win."

"Please."

"But you better be on the lookout 'cause it's on."

"Ooh," she taunted.

"You wanna make a bet on who can get more?"

"How about dinner?" she asked.

"You're on." It was perfect—Jackson couldn't take me to Sycamore Street that night anyway.

After an hour or so more of work, we decided to break for lunch. Kathy had brought lunches in her backpack. She'd carried the bag all morning without complaining about it or anything. She was pretty tough like that. When she took off the pack there was a giant sweat spot on her back. That was disgusting, but I couldn't blame her. I was pretty hot and sweaty myself.

"Thanks for the lunch," I said, biting into the ham sandwich. "And thanks for not putting the Dijon mustard on there." We were sitting beneath the shade of a cypress tree. There was a swamp nearby and although I was pretty concerned about gators, Kathy seemed to think we were safe. I ate facing the swamp so I could see if a predator emerged.

"You're welcome. And thanks ahead of time for dinner."

"Day's not over," I replied. She'd counted six sparrows, three times as many as me.

She put the uneaten half of her sandwich back in the

bag and stuffed it into her pack. "Will you pass me one of those napkins?"

I did.

"Remember the first time I met you?" I asked. "How I spilled all those napkins?"

She smiled.

"You didn't like me."

"You were okay. But I didn't really want to be seen with you," she said, still smiling.

"What's that supposed mean?"

"Seriously?" she asked.

"Yeah."

"Well, for starters, your pants were too short," she said.

"Flash floods are no joke."

"And you always had that deck of cards with you. It was weird."

"What's wrong with a deck of cards?" I pulled out my cards and held them up. "Some folks carry a newspaper, books. I carry cards."

"You know you have a problem when..." she mused.

"I *don't* have a problem."

She was smiling because she thought the conversation was all fun and games, but I didn't think it was funny or a game. I was serious. And I was getting seriously irritated.

"Getting expelled isn't a problem?" she asked.

"I was framed by your boyfriend, Hollis."

"Oh, okay," she said incredulously.

"This keeps coming up because you don't believe me!

And I don't even want to talk about it. I've told you that a thousand times, which is obviously not good enough. Maybe if my last name was Mulwray, you'd believe me."

"Are you serious?"

I didn't answer.

"I've known Hollis a lot longer than I've known you," she barked back. "And don't forget that half the class said that you were responsible for it, Jim."

"Hollis is rich, popular, and an upperclassman. It wasn't a hard choice."

"Y'know, Jim, not everything is someone else's fault," she said with a sigh, half turning away from me. "Sometimes you've just got to own up for what you've done."

"Shows how much you know."

I stormed away to take a piss. That settled why she didn't want to go out with me. She didn't trust me. To her, I was just a liar and a coward with a card-playing problem who blamed everything on Hollis.

By the time I zipped up, I wasn't angry anymore but depressed, on account of her being right: I was a liar who was untrustworthy, who took money from Aunt Mel to throw down in some half-cracked gambling ring on Sycamore Street.

I spent the next hour by myself not really counting sparrows 'cause I felt bad about my rotten luck and shitty life. Finally, I decided to find Kathy and apologize for getting so bent out of shape about all that crap we'd argued about. I told her I was sorry for being such a jerk. She said it was okay, but I could tell it had really bothered her.

"So how many sparrows have you counted?" I asked finally.

"Nine. And you?"

"Six," I told her.

"Really?"

"No," I said with a pleading smile. "I heard six. I saw four."

Later we turned in our report sheets to the really sweet Cuban guy with the curly dark hair who could kick my ass. He was pretty big, and Kathy was right: he could probably kick my ass if it came to that. I was standing by the door while Kathy flirted with Mr. Pablo Ellroy. She finally came and found me and was all bubbly and happy. That made me kinda sick. I didn't like that Ellroy guy one bit, with his rosy cheeks and sexy accent and his liberal agenda. I'm sure his political ambitions probably included Kathy as more than his running mate.

Twenty-nine

There must have been several hundred dollars worth of losing scratch-off tickets in the kitchen trash can. Although I knew that Aunt Mel was using our savings to buy baking ingredients for the cookies (she still hadn't seen the neighbors), I had no idea she was spending money on lottery tickets.

I'd taken a shower and put lotion on my sunburned face and was waiting for Kathy to swing back by and pick me up for dinner. Not that it was a date or anything—at least, I didn't think so. Not until Aunt Mel called out to me from the other room, asking if I was "nervous about my date."

"It's not a date," I replied as I closed the trash-can lid and walked into the living room.

"Yeah right, look at that nice shirt, not a date. You can't fool me," she said, smiling from fat ear to fat ear.

Like I said, I really didn't think it was a date.

"In my day," she said, "dinner with a girl was *always* a date."

And then cars were invented and dating concepts changed forever, I thought.

I anxiously started shuffling my cards again. I was nervous. Not so much about dinner, but whether or not to confront Aunt Mel about the money she was wasting on the baking stuff and the lottery tickets.

"You with those cards," Aunt Mel said, oblivious to how upset I was becoming. "You're not going to take those with you, are you?"

"I was going to."

Aunt Mel playfully snatched them away. "You don't want to do that, Jim. You want Kathy to have your full attention."

Like she should be talking, with her dating credentials. "Give them back," I said, standing up and walking over to her. She had moved to the kitchen and put the cards in a kitchen drawer.

"Nope."

"Goddamn it," I shouted. "Give them back!"

"Jim, you need to watch how you speak to me." She took the cards out of the drawer and slapped them into my palm. "I was just trying to help," she said. "But obviously you don't need any."

"No, I don't."

She went back into the living room, turned on the television, and started tying another dog toy.

So I just put my cards in my pocket and left without saying another word. I'd worked so hard for the little money we had, and she was just wasting it on stupid scratch-and-win tickets!

As I walked toward the front of the Straits to wait for Kathy I started to feel bad for Aunt Mel, sitting there in our trailer all alone with her dog toys.

I made it to the front gate just as Kathy was pulling in. She stopped her car next to me and I got in.

"I thought I was picking you up at your trailer?"

"I'm all sweaty now," I said. It was the truth, but I don't know why I said it. It didn't even answer her question.

Kathy was wearing this white linen dress. It was the prettiest thing I'd ever seen. Her hair was down to her shoulders and her body was tan. She really looked good. I started to forget about Aunt Mel.

"You look nice," I finally said, as we were walking across the parking lot toward the restaurant.

"Thanks," she said, blushing a little. "I feel frumpy."

We went to a little Italian restaurant that Kathy had been talking about all summer. It was the kind of kitschy, suburban place that sprouts up in a shopping center and then, within a year, it closes. The *grand opening* sign hangs in the window the whole time, and at first everyone thinks it's a terrific place because it's local and not a chain. Then four months later, everyone is back to the Olive Garden. And then it's doomsday for the little Italian restaurant with the kitschy art deco pictures and the fake plants.

I didn't say all that much during dinner because I was back to feeling guilty about being an asshole to Aunt Mel. Kathy kept asking me what was wrong, but how was I gonna tell her that I had yelled at Aunt Mel? So I just said nothing was wrong.

I paid for dinner like a goddamn gentleman. Kathy thanked me and smiled. She really looked good in that dress.

After we got to her car, she asked me once and for all what was wrong. "You've been distant all night."

"Sorry," I said, staring across the parking lot. "Maybe I'm just tired or something."

"We don't have to go get coffee. Do you want to just go home?"

"No."

"Are you sure? Because you're acting like it."

Honestly, I wanted to apologize to Aunt Mel more than anything and I wasn't going to be able to think straight until I'd done it. "Maybe we can get coffee tomorrow?" I asked.

She hesitated before saying that it was okay with her.

As my luck would have it, when Kathy dropped me off at home, Aunt Mel was asleep in bed. And then I got kinda sad because I had just ruined my date with Kathy, if you could call it that, to come home to a dark, sleepy trailer.

I wrote Aunt Mel a note and told her I was sorry for what I'd said. I left it on the kitchen counter and went for a walk to clear my head. I thought about going over the Jackson's house, but I knew he was doing the lame family thing for his brother's birthday.

I wished I had something lame like that to do.

When I got back home the note I'd left was gone and another note was there.

You're forgiven, Jim it said, in Aunt Mel's third grade penmanship.

SUNDAY MORNING, AUGUST 31

The National Hurricane Center issues a warning after tropical storm Theodore intensifies. Wind speeds exceed 74 mph and the storm is elevated to hurricane status. The speed and intensity of the storm is expected to increase throughout the day.

With storm surges as high as 15 feet, severe flooding and structure damage is a possibility if Hurricane Theodore turns westward.

City, state, and local officials are notified.

Thirty

I woke up and dragged myself over to Kathy's house. I needed to explain why I had been such a lame-ass the night before.

As I was walking through the Straits, I saw some men moving a couple of trailers out of the park. They were just unhooking the water pipes and everything, and hitching the trailers up and driving them away. It was strange, and made moving away seem more immediate. Even though the trailers were totally ghetto and all of that, I'd gotten used to them. I was scared that our next house might be worse than the Straits. I didn't want to be that homeless kid who was always with that old woman with the bike-helmet haircut who tied dog toys. I didn't want to end up like Mathers with the baseball-mitt face and the missing teeth.

When I got to Kathy's house, I knocked on the door. Mr. Montgomery answered. "Hey, Jim."

"Is Kathy around?"

"She is."

Kathy's backyard was pretty small. We were sitting on the deck drinking sweetened iced tea. It was a little too sweet for my liking, but I wasn't going to complain. The air was ripping hot. I was sweating just sitting there thinking about it. It had been raining a lot lately, on and off, on and off. We were under one of those giant table umbrellas—the kind you always find in the middle of the yard after a storm.

"It looks like it's going to rain again," I said.

"There's a hurricane off the coast. I heard it's not supposed to come inland, though."

"I hope not," I said as I took a sip of the sweet tea.

Kathy was in a foul mood. I could tell.

"What's wrong?" I asked.

"Nothing."

"Yeah, right."

She didn't say anything.

I said, "I'm sorry about bailing on the coffee last night."

"That's okay."

"Are you sure?"

She hesitated and then said, "Why didn't you tell me about the gambling, Jim?"

"About what?" I stuttered. I couldn't believe what I was hearing—how did she find out about that?

"You know what I'm talking about," she said.

It was a delicate situation. I didn't expect Kathy to understand. To begin with, not only had I kept the gambling from her, but she thought that poor folks like me shouldn't be gambling or drinking or smoking or doing any of the things you always see poor folks doing. She was real serious about it. She thought those vices just wasted the few resources that we had.

But Kathy wasn't poor. Her convictions didn't come from experience, but from books and classrooms and teachers and parents who didn't understand what it was like to be poor themselves. They didn't realize that forgetting that you were poor was sometimes more important than anything, escaping through a dream of winning the scratch-and-win or through alcohol or drugs or death ... or gambling. Their idealism told them that when escapism replaced hope, death was sure to follow. They didn't understand that sometimes dying poor-but-escaped wasn't so bad after all.

I couldn't look at her. "How'd you find out?" I asked.

"Does it really matter?"

"I don't know."

"Hollis told me last night. After I dropped you off, I met up with everyone at the Walking Jay."

"And he just told you?" I didn't know why I was so surprised. It was Hollis, after all.

"What does that have to do with you not telling me in the first place?" she snapped.

I took out my deck of cards and started shuffling them.

"Could you please stop doing that with the cards? While we're talking?"

"Why?"

"What is it with those cards? Y'know, maybe you should stop taking those cards everywhere. Maybe you're just holding on to the past or something..." She trailed off.

"They're just cards."

We were silent for a few minutes.

"We're supposed to be friends, Jim."

"We are," I said.

"Friends tell one another when they get fired from their jobs. And they don't lie about gambling down on Sycamore Street."

She sighed. And it kinda made my heart beat a little faster and sink a little lower. Because I saw where this conversation was going and I knew where it would come to an end.

"I'm not doing it for fun," I offered. "There's no other way to get the money we need in time."

She shook her head slowly. "Why didn't you tell me?"

"I just didn't want you think... that I was some kind of loser."

"I've never thought you were any kind of loser, Jim."

I was still having a hard time looking at her. I said, "Would you be saying that if you knew it was my fault that my mom and Martha were dead?"

She hesitated before saying, "You've never given me the chance. I don't know why you told yourself that, but it's not your fault they died in that hurricane any more than it's my fault my mom died of cancer."

"You weren't there."

I expected her to get up and go inside, but she just looked off into the distance. There wasn't a fence behind her house. The neighbors had a pool, and through the bushes and such that bordered the property line, you could make out their wet bodies slithering around in the water. They were being awfully loud swimming back there. I wished I was over there and I wished I was part of that family. But I wasn't over there, and I wasn't part of that family.

I took a big sip of iced tea, taking one of the ice cubes into my mouth, and then I spit it out on the ground.

She stood and folded her arms across her chest. She looked at me and then she looked away.

Then she sat back down across from me. I pretended to not be watching every little thing she did.

I got up and went and sat down next to her and started talking.

Thirty-one

I told Kathy about how my mom had gone to help Aunt Mel. How Martha and I hid in the closet. How, while my mom was gone, the two of us played cards by flashlight. (It distracted Martha from what the hell was really going on all around us.) I told Kathy how the roof suddenly ripped off, sending shards of wood and metal everywhere. How Martha somehow slipped away from me while we ran to the kitchen pantry. How I was sent to the car while my mom went inside to look for her.

I had done the wrong thing and betrayed and failed my mom and Martha, abandoning her when she needed me the most. I had watched helplessly, frozen while the electrical box and phone pole crashed down on the house, collapsing in a mess of sparks, splitting wood, and grinding metal.

I was standing, pacing around her deck nervously. Kathy was sitting down, leaning forward and resting her elbows on her knees. "The really sad and tragically ironic thing about it all," I said, "was that Aunt Mel had already made it to safety by the time my mom got over to her house. One of their neighbors had helped her, so my mom ended up going over there for nothing at all. Aunt Mel felt terrible after she learned about what happened. I think that's why she's so goddamn depressed all the time."

Kathy stood up and walked over to me. "It was one of the worst hurricanes in fifty years. You didn't kill them—the storm did."

I sat back down and then Kathy sat down next to me.

I wiped the tears from my eyes.

"Have you ever felt like everything you did was wrong?" I asked.

She nodded.

"Have you ever felt like you didn't even matter?"

"Of course you matter, Jim."

My tea glass was empty, but I picked it up and looked in it anyway.

"Why are you telling me this now?" she asked.

I put the glass down and stood up. "Because I like you. I always have."

I tried to look at Kathy. It was hard. It started to rain,

but Kathy and I were dry because of the umbrella. Actually, I was a little wet since water kept splashing off the deck and hitting me. But it didn't matter.

"Jim?" she finally said, standing up. She was facing away from me. Her arms were crossed again and she was holding her shoulders.

"Yeah?" I said.

"I don't think..." she trailed off.

When she started talking again, I could hear that her voice was trembling a little bit. "...I like to you too, but—"

"It's Hollis, isn't it?" I interrupted.

She sighed and shook her head, frustrated. "I knew you were going to say that."

"It's not?"

Kathy took forever to respond. And then she said, "I don't trust you, if you want to know the truth."

"What?"

"I mean, you've never been completely honest with me about anything. Not your mom. Not how you feel. Not about your job. Not about the... gambling."

"Did I not just tell you what happened in the storm? I've never told anyone that. And I just told you about the gambling," I said.

"It's a start," she replied quietly.

Thirty-two

I left Kathy's house in a huff and walked home in the rain. She'd offered to give me a ride but I declined, goddamnit. Sometimes it felt good to just be alone.

By the time I got to the Straits, it was storming pretty bad but I hardly noticed because I was fixated on how much I wanted to get Hollis back. Just kill him for telling Kathy about me getting fired and gambling on Sycamore Street.

I walked into the trailer. Although Aunt Mel was sitting upright with a half-tied dog toy in her hand, I could see she was napping. So I went into the kitchen and pulled out the savings can, taking the rest of the money and stuffing it into my pocket. I returned the can to the cabinet beneath the sink. Then I stood there for a minute in the creaky quietness of the trailer, leaning against the counter wondering whether or not I should go through with it…wondering whether there might be some other option.

"Jim, is that you?" Aunt Mel called.

"Yeah."

"Will you get me some water?"

I carried a glass of water into the living room and watched her slurp it down.

"There's a hurricane heading up the coast," she said when she was finished.

I didn't answer 'cause I didn't feel like it.

"What's wrong?" she asked.

"Nothing, I just hate this trailer," I said, flopping down on the sofa.

Aunt Mel smiled. "I won't miss this place either. Not one bit."

I didn't feel like talking about anything. Which I reckon made me look like I wanted to listen, because Aunt Mel then said, "Y'know, I've practically *lived* at that window twenty-four hours a day. I've been feeding them my special cookies and I still haven't seen them. Not once."

"Maybe they don't exist," I blurted out. "It's not like anybody matters in here. Not the Rodriguezes, not the Vargases, not the people across the street, Aunt Mel. I reckon not even us."

"Don't say 'reckon,'" she said. "Your mother wouldn't

have liked it. Now," she began, "'are not two sparrows sold for a penny? Yet not one of them will fall to the ground apart from the will of your Father. And even the very hairs of your head are all numbered. So don't be afraid; you are worth more than many sparrows.' That's in Matthew. And that's what I have to believe, Jim. I just have to."

"Well, what the hell does Matthew know. I don't even have a father."

"They put him in the Bible, so he must know something," she replied, glancing at the empty glass in her hands.

I wanted to ask Aunt Mel why some folks like Hollis Mulwray had all the luck. Why everything worked out perfectly for them even though they didn't deserve it. I wanted to ask her why folks like us, who worked hard and tried to do everything right, still got the short end of the stick, the low card, the bad beat. Why we had to struggle to make ends meet when the assholes of the world got to live free and easy.

I didn't ask her any of those things.

Aunt Mel finally said, "You've worked so hard at your job, which I know hasn't been easy when you could have just given up. Your mom and sister would've been very proud of you, Jim. So don't go telling me that you don't matter, that you're not making a difference."

"Big deal," I said. I stood and walked over to the phone to call Jackson, to find out what time I was meeting him to go gambling one final time on Sycamore Street.

Thirty-three

left the trailer and on the way over to the Walking Jay, I got to thinking about what Matthew said and about Aunt Mel. I figured she was so intent on seeing those people in the trailer across the field because if she could see them, they could see her, and in that way she'd know—even though she was living in the Straits—that she existed, that she mattered. And I also thought that just like those goddamn sparrows or planets or hairs on my head, it was the same with cards—each one meant something, even the two of clubs.

As I got nearer the parking lot of the Walking Jay, I came upon Mathers walking in the opposite direction.

"Jim!"

"Hey, Mathers."

"Yep, terrific." He must have thought I asked him how he was doing.

"Where you going?" I asked.

"Home. There's hurricane coming."

I could tell Mathers had been drinking. His head wouldn't stay still and his eyes were kinda bobbling there, like apples in a barrel. "Better get to high ground!" he shouted, laughing to himself unceremoniously, almost ruefully.

"Where's home, Mathers?"

He scratched his head, looked around, and then laughed and said, "I don't remember. But I think Bobby is picking me up tonight."

"Is Bobby your son?"

"Yep."

First of all, I didn't think there was going to be a hurricane. During storm season, sabers rattled at every rainstorm—it was a Florida pastime. Second, I knew Mathers didn't have a son. Third of all, he was pretty tanked, so I didn't think he knew what was happening or what he was saying or where he was going.

"Is that who you live with—Bobby?"

"Yep."

"Where?"

He arbitrarily pointed somewhere off behind the gas station. "In the darkness on … the edge of down," he said, smiling from ear to ear.

"Town?" I offered.

"Yep, just like everyone else."

"Have you been drinking?" I asked, already knowing the answer.

He thought about it long and hard. Finally he said, "Yep."

"Maybe you should go inside and get some coffee and sober up. You don't look so good."

"I'd rather go home," he said. "Can you help me?"

I didn't have time. Jackson was going to be picking me up soon.

"Where do you live?" I asked.

"Not far. Maybe a mile or two or three or four..."

"Why don't you just go inside for a while," I offered, gently taking his arm.

He yanked his arm away. "No!"

I was starting to lose patience. "It's gonna rain again soon, Mathers. You don't want to be out in the rain."

"I like the rain." He withdrew a bottle of whiskey from somewhere in his jacket and took a swig. "Now, are you going to help me or what?"

"I can't, Mathers. I'm meeting someone here in a few minutes."

"Thanks for nothing, then," he said matter-of-factly. "I thought we were friends."

Mathers was really starting to bother me.

"I'm out here trying to help you!" he added.

"No you're not," I snapped. "You're acting like the crazy

bum everyone says you are." I don't know why I said it. I regretted it immediately. In a way, it proved his point—what kind of friend says that to another?

Just then, from across the parking lot, Mathers caught sight of some man wearing a NASA hat. Without a second drunken thought, he stumbled over to him. I just stood there watching Mathers walk, all crooked and tipsy. Of course, the guy in the NASA hat brushed him to the side, practically shoving him to the ground. And all Mathers wanted to do was talk about space and stuff. I felt awfully bad for Mathers. He was all alone, drunk, talking about a hurricane that wasn't coming and a son he didn't have.

I was sitting in Kathy's favorite booth sipping a cup of coffee when I saw Jackson speed his station wagon into the parking lot at five miles per hour. He parked right in front. As I went out to meet him, a red sports car pulled up alongside me.

Hollis was driving. Jesse Danner was stuffed in the back. He looked stupid back there because he was peeking his head forward between the two front seats, kinda like a dog looks out a doggy door to check on the weather. I didn't know why he wasn't riding in the front seat.

"Is there something we can do for you?" Jackson asked as Hollis got out of his car and leaned against it, folding his arms across his chest.

"I don't know, *ith* there?" Jesse lisped in. You could

just tell he was starving to be in the conversation, to be part of the action. Like the dog in the doggy door.

I was standing on the opposite side of the station wagon from where Hollis had pulled up.

"Shut up," Hollis barked at Jesse.

Jesse sat back, dejected. Jackson got out of his car.

"What do you want, Hollis?" I asked, lighting one of Jackson's cigarettes. I really wanted to punch his lights out for telling Kathy about Sycamore Street.

"You're going to Sycamore tonight, right?"

"Yeah," Jackson snapped.

"Then I want to end this once and for all," Hollis said.

"End what?" I demanded.

He just smiled and said that Kathy was totally on the verge of going out with him, if I would stop interfering and putting thoughts in her head.

"Kathy can think for herself. She's just way too good for you," I said.

"You've got it backwards."

"That's some pure bullshit," Jackson volunteered.

Hollis stepped away from his car and approached me so that he was standing inches from my face. "You wanna bet?"

"Yeah, we do," Jackson said.

"Shut up," snapped Hollis.

"Say that again," Jackson threatened. "Tell me to shut up again."

I told Jackson to chill out and then turned back to Hollis. "What do you have in mind?"

"If I win, you stay away from Kathy."

"And if I win?"

"What do you want?" he asked.

"Admit to Kathy that you set me up at the Academy."

"Gladly," he said. "Is that all?"

I didn't know what else to ask for, and then it came to me. "And I want your car."

He hesitated for a moment. But only for a moment. "You're on." He stepped back. "I'll see you two chumps there."

Jackson went up to Hollis' car and mockingly rubbed the top. "Boy, I can't wait to ride around in this thing."

"Shut up and get your paws off my car, Smiles."

Jackson's hand jerked self-consciously toward his mouth before he caught himself. Then he methodically went to the back of the station wagon and pulled out a tire iron. Hollis saw what he was doing and jumped in his car and peeled out. Hollis got away, but not before Jackson got a good, clean swipe at the car, barely missing the rear window.

Hollis sped across the parking lot and drove away. Jackson chased him on foot as far as I could see, yelling obscenities and waving the tire iron. I didn't know why Jackson ran after him so far, because it's not like he was actually going to catch him.

When Jackson got back, he was sweaty and out of

breath. "I didn't catch them," he said. I just stared at him for a second and then I started laughing. And then he started laughing.

Thirty-four

So this is the last night."

"It has to be. Tomorrow is September 1st."

We drove in silence for a while. I glanced at Jackson. It was obvious he had something else on his mind.

"Well, I do want to see Hollis get what's coming to him," he finally said.

"But?"

"But just don't let getting him back get in the way of the money you and Aunt Mel need to move out of the Straits. That's the most important thing. That's why we've been doing this in the first place, remember? Not to stick it to Hollis, but to get you some money."

I didn't like Jackson telling me what I already knew. "I know, Jackson. Thanks for pointing out the obvious."

"I'm just trying to look out for you," he said.

"Thanks, but I don't need your help."

We didn't talk the rest of the way to the house on Sycamore Street.

Thirty-five

It was raining something fierce outside and the wind was really picking up, too. But all I cared about were my two pocket cards in front of me and Hollis' two cards in front of him.

It was around midnight. Everyone had bowed out, gracefully or ungracefully (the guy in the sunglasses and hat was pretty pissed), and I found myself right where I wanted to be: in a heads-up duel with Hollis Mulwray. I hadn't had a great hand all night, so I was due for one. For chrissakes, I'd only been dealt a couple of top pair and the flops weren't doing a damn thing for me. But in spite of my pocket cards, I'd done pretty well bluffing or buying pots from some of the guys. And I'd slowly pecked away at Hollis' chip count, all because he more or less kept mucking his cards if he didn't think he was going to win. I exploited his deficiencies all the way to the bank and turned my several hundred dollars into about $4,000. Almost all of that money had come from Hollis alone.

I was the big blind and Robert dealt me a 9♥ and an A♣ in the pocket. The flop came with a 2♦, an A♥, and a 9♣.

"Cheepo. This'll be interesting," Cheepo said. "Cheepo thinks this is going to break someone."

When Hollis called my decent-size preflop raise, I should've known something was going on. I didn't think he could beat my two pair and I thought maybe, just maybe, he was bluffing for once. Before the turn, I led out with a big raise, about $1,000, thinking I'd scare him off, but he called. Maybe he had found a pair with the ace or the nine. Or it was possible that he'd flopped a straight. Perhaps he had a set (three of a kind) if he was dealt a pair in the pocket. I'd find out on the next card.

A 6♦ came up on the turn. That probably didn't help either of us and we both knew it. But Hollis sighed and glanced around the room. He immediately started looking at his chips and then gave me a challenging stare. I thought he was acting confident to throw me off. When folks act confident, they're usually bluffing.

"What do you got?" he asked, taunting.

Jackson was nervously pacing back and forth over near the wall. He stopped and looked at me.

I stared at Hollis with no expression on my face. I figured my odds, crossed my fingers, and thought *to hell with it*. "All in," I said calmly.

I had $4,000 in the pot. I felt as confident as I had ever felt in a game of Texas Hold'em. But if I'd been playing against anyone other than my current opponent, I can assure you that I wouldn't have pushed $4,000 in blue, white, red, and green chips into the middle of the table. I wouldn't have gone all in…well, maybe. I knew that if I lost, not only would Aunt Mel and I have hardly any money left, but I'd never be able see Kathy again. Yet if I won, I'd silence Hollis Mulwray once and for all—taking his money and his car in the process.

I decided to go with the numbers. The numbers said I had a pretty good chance of winning.

Everything was riding on this hand. And everything was better than nothing.

Hollis sat across from me, scrutinizing the cards as if they were some kind of riddle to be solved. He was biting his bottom lip and trying to make it look casual. He wasn't trying hard enough, that's for sure.

"Do you see what Jim just did, Cliff?" Cheepo squeaked.

"I do have one good eye, Cheepo!" Cliff said with a laugh.

Banana Jack took of his hat and wiped the sweat from his brow with a handkerchief.

It was taking a long time for Hollis to make up his mind about what to do. The longer he took, the more nervous I got.

Robert looked from me to Hollis. Cliff used his eye to look from me to Banana Jack to Cheepo to Hollis.

"I hope you know what you're doing, Jim," Jackson said from somewhere behind me.

As Hollis deliberated, chewing on his lip and looking foolish as always, I tried to occupy my mind with all the ways I was going to spend the money and where I was going to drive Kathy in Hollis' sports car. With all the places I could find a new job...

And then all of a sudden I got nervous, really nervous. From the depths of my stomach, I felt a self-loathing and dread and anxiety rise and overcome me like an ocean wave upon a sandy beach. It was something that I hadn't felt in a long time, not since my mom and sister had died. What had I done? It was our entire savings. I needed that money. Aunt Mel needed that money. Our livelihood depended on it. I'd risked everything, on what? Two pair? Maybe I could take it back. Maybe nobody would care, maybe they would think it was an honest—

"Call," he said calmly, as he pushed all his chips into the pot.

—mistake.

Someone said, "Show 'em." I don't remember who it was because I was sort of not in the moment. And at the same time, strangely in it and overwhelmed by it. Like when you go on one of those roller coasters and you crest that big-ass hill that's always right at the beginning of the ride. Just before you plunge straight down at a thousand miles per hour, there is a second or two when everything kinda freezes and you realize how idiotic riding a stupid roller coaster is and how pathetic it would be to die on one. And just as you think that the ride needs to be stopped because *your* seat belt is the only one broken—whoosh, it's too late. That's what I was thinking and that was how I felt as Hollis slowly spread his two cards down on the table...6♣...2♥...

That gave him two pair. More importantly, that gave him bottom pair, which meant that the odds of me winning were really good.

I flipped over my cards, and stood up.

"Shit," Hollis muttered angrily.

Cheepo let out this high-pitched cackle.

"Two pair for Hollis," Robert announced. "Jim's got top pair. The only way for Hollis to win is to catch a full house on the river."

"Shit, Jim! I'll be damned," cried Banana Jack.

While I was sure I was going to win, gloating and bragging weren't really my thing. And I knew enough to see that river could wash away my fortune in an instant.

"You girls ready?" Robert said in a careful voice. He looked to me and looked to Hollis. "Good luck."

Robert turned the river—and it was 2♣.

Thirty-six

With a full house, Hollis had won all my money and my promise to cut ties with Kathy. I couldn't believe it.

My stomach turned over and fell through the floor. It took me a couple of seconds to register what had happened, but it didn't take nearly that long for Hollis to realize he'd won. He jumped up and cheered. His chair fell back and slid across the floor. While he was hooting and howling, Cheepo said, "That's a bad beat, Jim."

"You had him," Banana Jack added.

"And then you lost him," concluded Cliff.

Jackson sank into the chair next to me. He mumbled obscenities to himself. And I couldn't take my eyes away from the table. I just stared at the cards. I just stared at my two aces and my two nines and his three twos and two sixes ...

Thirty-seven

We didn't go home right away. Jackson drove around and around because I asked him to.

"I don't want to go home," I'd said, making no attempt to hide the emptiness in my voice.

"Yeah," he'd replied drearily.

It was all either of us said.

So he just drove and drove. And I rode and rode.

Although the night was stormy, my mind felt empty, still, and silent—I was alone on the bottom of the deep, dark ocean. I stared out the car window, feeling more depressed than I did when I got fired. There were no more ways to make any money and there was no more time in which to make it.

I had lost all our savings to the biggest asshole in the world. What was Aunt Mel going to do when she found out? Or Kathy? I didn't let Jackson see, but I let my head fall against the cold, cold window and closed my eyes. I wanted my mind to go blank, to forget all of my troubles, but it wouldn't and my stomach hurt. I reckon that was a punishment I deserved for being so stupid and for doing everything wrong.

Jackson lit a cigarette. Out of the corner of my eye, I saw the flick of his red lighter and then I could hear him toss it onto the dashboard. It bounced off and landed on the floor. Neither of us made any move to pick it up.

The rain was falling hard and fast against the windshield, but I didn't hear anything. The wind was really tearing around the car, blowing the station wagon across the lines in the road. But I didn't hear a thing. There weren't any cars out. None. I didn't see a single vehicle, coming or going, on our way home. But neither of us said anything about it. We were still thinking about that gut shot served up by the river.

What was I going to do? How could I possibly tell Aunt Mel? What was she going to say?

How disappointed she was.

How I just couldn't do anything right.

How I would never amount to anything.

How I just didn't matter.

When Jackson dropped me off at the trailer, I just sat on the front steps in the wind and torrential rain, crying to myself. I just couldn't hold it in any longer. Since the moment I lost to Hollis there'd been a big pounding in my chest I'd been trying to ignore. The moment Jackson drove away, it just exploded into a mess of tears. It felt like a lifetime ago that I had been working at Mulwray Construction. A lifetime ago that I was in school at the Academy. A lifetime ago that I felt happy. What was I going to do? I'd hurt or betrayed everyone—my mom, Martha, Aunt Mel, and Kathy. Even when Mathers asked for help, I completely disregarded him.

After a few minutes, I got hold of myself and stood up to go inside to face Aunt Mel. That's when a car pulled up and screeched to a halt. It was Kathy. The thought actually crossed my mind that since it was raining and my face was wet, she wouldn't be able to tell whether I was crying or not.

Kathy jumped out of her car and ran up to me. The rain had matted down her hair, which was covering her face. She pulled it back so that she could see.

"What're you doing here?" I asked. I had to yell, it was so loud.

"Have you seen Hollis?"

"Is this a trick question?"

"Everyone is looking for him! His family has been trying to find him for hours."

"Why?"

"Are you kidding?"

"Huh?"

"It's a hurricane, Jim! It's been all over the news! They've issued a state of emergency!"

"So what're you doing here? I mean, where's your dad?"

"He's with the Mulwrays!"

"And he just let you leave?"

"Not exactly. Do you know where Hollis is?"

"We were playing cards on Sycamore Street!"

"And he was there when you left?"

I nodded, wiping the water from my face. I was really getting drenched and so was Kathy. She turned and ran back to her car. I followed her. "Where are you going?"

"To find him!"

I got in the car.

Kathy was driving as recklessly as you can imagine, given that we were in the middle of a hurricane and I was trying to save the person who'd just ruined my life. She wasn't too pleased to learn that I wasn't supposed to see her anymore.

"You bet what?"

"I thought I was going to win."

"You guys don't control who my friends are."

I didn't know what to say. She was right.

"And what were you thinking?"

I shrugged helplessly and pulled out my pack of cigarettes,

but they were soaked. I tossed them out the window as Kathy veered around a fallen tree that was blowing like a torpedo through the brown, white-capped water on the road. "Shit!" I yelled, grabbing the roof of the car.

"Calm down."

"You're dad's going to kill you," I said. "If you don't do it first."

"I know."

Thirty-eight

I knew it wasn't going to be easy and it was most definitely not going to be safe. Sure, it was raining like hell and the wind was blowing and I saw a stop sign flying through the air like a Frisbee and I couldn't hear shit, but I reckon if I was lost or missing, I would want someone to come looking for me.

We had parked and gotten out of the car to find that Sycamore Street was totally flooded. The water was rushing in from nearby Lake Chadwick and the confluence tributary, both of which, in the time since I'd left the Sycamore Street neighborhood, had overflowed. And the water was rising pretty fast. You could smell gasoline and sewage coming from somewhere.

Kathy and I were attempting to stand on the last bit of ground before it gave way to the windswept water. It didn't look too deep, but there was no way to tell 'cause it was so dark and dirty-looking. The rain was coming down sideways. The gusty wind was just like it was during Hurricane Leland—violent and unrelenting. I couldn't believe that Kathy and I were about to go trudging down Sycamore Street to try and find Hollis Mulwray—the one person in the world who I thought deserved whatever he had coming.

I took a step, and suddenly I fell straight down, disappearing into a black, watery pit. At first I didn't know what had happened. But I figured it out pretty quick, let me tell you. We were in the middle of Sycamore Street, so there was only one kind of hole I could possibly plummet into—a manhole. When the water levels rose, the pressure must have pushed off the cover. Thank god that Kathy grabbed my hand because if she didn't, I could have easily drifted away from the opening and drowned in a subterranean water-grave.

Kathy held me up just enough for me to grab the side and hoist myself back to my feet. As I got up and caught my breath, two things occurred to me in rapid succession. One, that it naturally followed that I would find the one manhole without a lid, and two, that I would fall into it.

"Are you okay?"

"What're the chances?" I yelled, smiling just a little.

"That's not funny!"

Since Kathy wasn't in the mood to consider the odds of me falling into a manhole, we continued on our way, deciding it was best to try to walk along the sidewalk from that point on. No point in pushing my luck.

We made it to the driveway and hurried up toward the house. Hollis' car was nowhere to be seen.

"I don't see his car," I said. In fact, there were no cars around at all. It was completely deserted.

"But this is where you saw him last?" she asked impatiently.

"I don't know. Maybe he saw the hurricane and left," I shouted.

"Don't be an asshole."

"Okay, well. What should we do?"

She thought about it. "I don't know where else he could be. And we've come this far. I'm going in."

I wasn't happy about going in there, but I wasn't about to go wait in the car while Kathy went searching for him.

She followed me around to the back of the house.

I felt like I was about to get lifted and carried away by the wind. Literally. I mean, shit was flying through the air, smashing into houses and trees and splashing in the water. It was mostly trash and tree branches.

We went inside and it wasn't that much quieter. But I could hear myself think, at least.

"I think we should split up!" Kathy said.

"I don't think so!"

"We don't have much time. We have to!" she shouted. By the look on her face, I could tell she wasn't going to be convinced otherwise.

"Fine!"

"I'll start with the upstairs. You start down here!"

"Okay," I said, giving her the thumbs up because that was really the first time in my life that giving the thumbs up actually seemed fitting, and I was glad not to be going up those rickety stairs.

Staying low, I started looking around the first floor. I was hunched over, moving about carefully to avoid the windows and that sort of thing. There was about an inch of water across the floor, but it really didn't matter because I was drenched to the bone anyway.

I'd never really taken the time to look around the house before. Sure, I'd noticed this room or that room, but I'd never fully explored it. Even though I was trying to hurry, I couldn't help noticing how sinister it all was. The broken furniture. The branches sticking in through the windows. For the first time, I noticed the peeling wallpaper, the design of which kinda looked like hearts and spades and clubs and diamonds.

I imagined that the house was probably the most beautiful on the block once. I'm sure that back in the day, there were little kids running around, swinging on the banister, swimming in what's now the cesspool out back, playing piano in the family room, watching television in the den.

Not anymore. Just wind and rain in the darkness on the edge of town.

And then I realized I was standing in front of the kitchen pantry. I was just holding the door. Not turning the knob, not pulling or pushing. Just standing. Somewhere in the back of my mind, I thought that maybe I would open the door and Martha would be there waiting, and she would grab my shoulders and pull me down to her level and we would sit, hugging one another until my mother came and got us.

But that wasn't going to happen.

I opened the door to the pantry and it wasn't the pantry but a staircase leading down into the basement—the weeping belly of the beastly house. And then I sure wished it were a pantry after all, because I did not like the idea of going down into this hell-house basement of broken dreams by myself.

I slowly went down the stairs. There wasn't a railing, so I kinda used the wall to keep my balance. Each step seemed to creak and crack and yawn. I thought the stairs were going to collapse at any second. But they didn't.

The basement was starting to flood, and it smelled metallic and rotten. Water dripped from the upper levels, seeping through the cracks and corners and creases and splashing onto the concrete floor. And down on the floor was Hollis, hog tied, squirming and sprawled out on a worktable. Like some captured animal.

He was practically in tears and looking pathetic. Even

though I was there to save his life, the truth was that I still wanted to punch him.

"I didn't realize there was a basement down here," I said.

"Jim!" Hollis cried. "Get me outta here!"

"What happened?" I asked as I went over to him.

"Robert stole my car and my money!"

"You mean you lost it all?"

"No! It was after everyone left," Hollis shouted as I helped him get one arm free. He started working on another knot. "I had all this money and then Robert just turned on me. He took everything."

"Where'd he go?"

"How the hell should I know?"

"I wonder if the cops were onto him?"

As soon as I got Hollis untied enough to run, he bolted for the stairs. He didn't even thank me.

And I was right behind him.

But by the time I got to the kitchen, Hollis was heading out the front doors.

I caught up to him on the driveway. I think the hurricane was in full effect. We could barely even stand up straight because the wind was blowing so hard.

"Where's the car?" he yelled.

"On the hill," I shouted, pointing. "Just off Barrier!"

Suddenly there was a huge crash. Even over the wind, you could hear it. Part of the house had collapsed. Part of the third story, into the second story. And then I saw

Kathy through a detached abutment in an upstairs window, crying for help. Hollis and I both saw her. And I'm sure she saw both of us.

I looked at Hollis and then back to Kathy.

The house bent and cawed again and the roof above the porch broke free, slamming down with a splash and blocking the front door. I didn't ask myself if there was enough time to save her because, goddamnit, I wasn't going stand there and do nothing—not again.

Thirty-nine

I ran around back, making sure to keep my head low. "Through here!" I yelled. I looked back and saw that Hollis wasn't behind me like I thought he was.

Forgetting about him, I jumped in through the back doors and ran toward the front of the house, where the stairs were. But the stairs were gone. I went back outside. Climbing up onto the fallen part of the roof, I slowly made my way up the steep and slick incline of the tile. I got to the second floor and shimmied in through one of the windows.

Inside, I found what was left of the stairs and headed up, slowly, carefully to the third floor. I could see all the way down into the basement. With each step the stairs felt more precarious, more unsteady and shaky. I could feel my legs beginning to seize up and my chest begin to contract. My breathing was heavy and hard and I felt sick. It was my fear of heights. My fear of falling.

I felt my mind counting the steps—five, six, seven—even though I hadn't intended to. Eight, nine, ten ... I held on to the railing even though it wasn't giving me much comfort. Twelve, thirteen ... I was almost to the top when suddenly I felt the stairs begin to give way beneath me. I lunged clumsily and somehow managed to barely snag part of the banister. I could hear the set of stairs cracking and ricocheting off the wall as it fell down into the lower depths of the house.

I wasn't thinking of anything as I pulled myself up onto the floor. There was a sharp pain on my side where a wood shard had cut into my stomach. Blood was seeping through my shirt.

Then I didn't feel any pain.

I ran down the hall and into the master bedroom. In the corner, next to window, Kathy was trapped. Her foot had fallen through a gaping crack and become lodged in the floor.

"Jim! Thank god."

"Are you okay?" I asked, running over to her.

"Where's Hollis?"

"I don't know!"

Kathy's ankle was bleeding badly—something had sliced through her skin.

"Does it hurt? Because it looks like it hurts."

"Can we discuss this later?"

I grabbed a chair and used the leg to hammer away at the portion of the floor that was trapping her foot.

"I know you don't want to hear this right now," I said as I pushed against the inverted chair leg. "But I'm sorry. I'm sorry for not telling you the truth. About the gambling. About screwing up everything."

She smiled up at me. "Let's just hurry," she said.

The extraction went pretty smoothly, all considered, and we were off. Kathy was in front of me, faster than me even with her injury. I was really out of shape. I needed to quit smoking, I thought.

I stopped in the doorway to take one last look at the gambling room that had provided me with a small taste of success and the utter sting of failure. Over the past few days, the room had been both a gift and a curse. The room where I spent hours smoking cigarettes and playing cards. Trying to make a difference, to mean something, to matter.

The little table in the corner was on its side. There were several broken beer bottles. The cooler was still there. The huge table was a little off-kilter, away from the wall, and the ashtrays on it were filled with water. There were cigarette butts everywhere. The chairs were scuttled about.

I reckon my one last look took a little too long 'cause

suddenly the floor beneath me gave way. I fell and hit my head, and kept falling and falling, and then I was flying...

Forty

Flying so high over the house on Sycamore Street. It was the strangest and the greatest and most frightening experience. I was aware of what was happening, but I didn't quite comprehend it.

So up and up I went. From falling through the floor, from the third story of the house down through the second story, through the first story and into the basement, to soaring through the storm sort of like a bird. Actually, it was *just* like a bird. The wind was still blowing—I could see the trees bending at their trunks, the branches violently shaking.

It was the middle of night, but I could see clear as day.

I was high above, and down below, I could see Hollis making his way over to Kathy's car.

What a bastard, I thought.

I flew past the car and kept going, and then something really strange happened. I was over the Lake Hales Nature Preserve. Just like that. And there were sparrows, flying right alongside me. We weren't in any formation or anything, but we were flying ... together somehow.

Over the Wilmots' house between the beach and the golf course. The waves were crashing violently against the shore. The water had risen considerably, covering up most of the beach. The Wilmots' house, on stilts, was okay even though the water came so high up. I looked in the house as if the walls were not even there. But I didn't see anyone. Not Russ. Not any of his siblings. Not Mr. and Mrs. Wilmot. The house was completely deserted.

I sure hoped I didn't fly by the Mulwrays' house, where Mr. Montgomery would be worrying himself sick about Kathy and Mr. and Mrs. Mulwray would be flipping out about Hollis. That's not something I wanted to see. I felt bad that they were worrying about their kids. It might be worth it if I could communicate with them. I would tell them where Kathy was and where Hollis was. I would tell them that they were all right. But I didn't go by the Mulwrays' house.

I blinked and I was suddenly above Jackson's dirty old house. I could see his family through a window, all together in the living room. They were sitting by candlelight. It looked like they were all talking at once, having a good time. Just what you would expect from a family. I saw that old whale of a station wagon, parked up by the garage—it practically took up the entire driveway, the beast.

And then I soared above the Walking Jay. Roy had nailed boards over the windows and there were sandbags around a designated perimeter of the main building, which was up on a hill so the sandbags were really completely unnecessary. But like I said, Roy was crazy.

Then I was flying above the Straits, looking down. The trailers all looked like little white rectangles, all set out and ordered like points on a grid, equidistant from one another. And then I swooped real low to the ground and I was flying down "A" Road.

There were no lights on in any of the trailers. When I got near our trailer, I saw Aunt Mel still looking out the front window. And then I saw what she was looking at— Hollis' car, which was parked in front of the mysterious trailer at the edge of the field, near the trees. And then I saw who was living there—Mathers and Robert!

Suddenly, it all made sense. While Robert was off managing his floating parlor racket, his father, Mathers, was gallivanting around the Walking Jay, snacking on Aunt Mel's cookies and creeping everyone out.

I glanced back at Aunt Mel. Even though she appeared to be scared shitless, she looked satisfied.

The neighbors existed.

Aunt Mel existed.

Robert was running into the trailer and Mathers was withdrawing several stacks of cash from somewhere in the car, stuffing them into our Tupperware container. He stumbled across the field to our trailer and stuck the container between the screen door and the storm door. And I thought that was real goddamn generous of Mathers, to give Aunt Mel and me some of that money, especially after I didn't help him and called him a crazy bum. Just then, Robert ran out of the trailer with an armful of stuff and threw it in the trunk of the car. They both got in, then they drove away and they were gone forever.

As the wind and the rain continued, I flew from the Straits to South Ambricourt High. And then I was above the Andersons' house. (They had repaired the damage I'd done to the backyard. It looked nice. So did their new driveway, for that matter.) And then I was above Mulwray Construction headquarters. And then I was above Ambricourt Academy. It was there that I slowly stopped flying and just kinda came to a halt, hovering above the school.

I don't know how long I was there, but as I looked down at the Academy, Martha and I were waiting for my mom on the playground. She exited the school and approached us, calling out our names. I chased Martha to our car and we all got in and drove away. I started flying again, following the car as it drove along the street.

It was so goddamn strange. It was still in the present—the hurricane was destroying everything—but I was also in the past, following behind my mom, Martha, and me in the past as we drove home from school to our old house.

When we got there, Martha and I piled out and ran inside.

And then time slowly transformed and rolled forward. I could see that it was no longer some random school day, but the horrible day that they died.

I could somehow see Martha and me in the closet. I hugged her and we got out and ran through the house. Martha tripped and fell—something I hadn't noticed as I was *living* the experience.

I saw my mom pull up in her car. I ran out to her.

My mom hurried inside to find Martha, and when she did, she grabbed and hugged her. That was just before the telephone pole crashed in on top of the kitchen.

And in that moment, something became clear—that no matter whether I lived in the Straits or on some distant, newly-discovered planet, that no matter what I did or didn't do, no matter how many ways I found or invented to screw up everything I did, I meant something and I would always mean something. I realized that Mathers was right about a lot of things—that in life, everything and everyone matters. I mean, it was just like Aunt Mel and Matthew from the Bible said, people were important and worth living and dying for.

And suddenly, I began flying up again. And I was glad about that. I was glad I was leaving that experience behind.

I flew up and up and up, high above the hurricane. Through the rain and into the darkness. And beyond this strange darkness was a pain in my leg and in my head. And Kathy and Jackson's voices, oddly enough.

Forty-one

I opened my eyes to discover that I was in the basement, lying on the floor. I heard footsteps, and Jackson and Kathy came into view from the stairway.

"What happened?" I asked.

Kathy brushed my hair from my eyes.

"You fell through the floor."

I felt my head. It was throbbing like hell.

"You must have hit your head pretty hard," Kathy added.

"Feels like it." I thought of the flight through the storm over Ambricourt, over the Straits, and back in time to when my mom and Martha died. "Have I been here the whole time?"

"Where else would you have gone?"

"Nowhere, I reckon." I didn't understand it—how could I be soaring over Ambricourt one second and lying here, dripping wet and in pain, the next?

I looked down at my leg, which was in a splint. "Is it broken?"

"No doubt," Jackson said.

"Where'd I get the splint?"

"I made it for you," Kathy told me.

"When?"

"During the night."

"You stayed?"

"I wasn't going to leave you," she said.

"Wait, what happened to Hollis?" I asked.

"He's fine," Kathy said, "but we need to get you to a hospital."

I looked at Jackson. "Where'd you come from?"

"After the storm passed, I went by the trailer. Mel was freaking out because you weren't there. I mean, she was hysterical, waving dog toys around. And she kept saying something about some money. Said something about the neighbors paying her money for her cookies? God, she's really crazy, Jim."

"I know," I said with a smile.

"So I figured you might be here," he said.

"Good guess."

Jackson helped me to my feet and up the stairs and outside to his station wagon. The air was cool and gray and the clouds in the sky were thin and intermittent, outlined in a distant morning glow. He opened the hatch door and slid me onto the rear seat.

We pulled out of the driveway. If the neighborhood had looked like hell before, it looked even worse now. The flooded street was covered in branches, leaves, and various objects like orange traffic cones and some shopping bags and a roller skate. I wondered what the rest of Ambricourt looked like.

And then I reached in my pocket for my deck of cards. It was gone. It must have fallen out while I was in the house. Strangely, I felt okay about it.

Kathy looked at me. I smiled, and she leaned in and kissed me on the mouth. She said, "Thank you for coming back for me."

I wasn't really listening to her because I was thinking about the kiss.

Kathy put her hand in mine. And as Jackson slowly steered his station wagon down Sycamore Street and onto Barrier Avenue, I felt good for the first time in a very, very long time. Even as I was facing backwards, looking out the rear window at the storm wreckage … a spiral of smoke rising in the hazy, humid distance, scattered debris, and floating sewage and garbage lopping up and down in foamy skeins at the water's edge, goddamnit.

The End

About the Author

Jeremy Craig is a graduate student in the film program at Columbia University. He lives in New York City with his wife. This is his first novel.